Heroine of the *Titanic*

Heroine
of the *Titanic*

The Real Unsinkable Molly Brown

Elaine Landau

Clarion Books   New York

Clarion Books
a Houghton Mifflin Company imprint
215 Park Avenue South, New York, NY 10003
Copyright © 2001 by Elaine Landau

Book design by Lisa Diercks.
The type was set in 13-point Bembo.

www.houghtonmifflinbooks.com

Printed in the U.S.A.

Library of Congress Cataloging-in-Publication Data

Landau, Elaine.
Heroine of the Titanic : the real unsinkable Molly Brown / by Elaine Landau.
p. cm.
Includes bibliographical references.
ISBN 0-395-93912-7
1. Brown, Margaret Tobin, 1867–1932. 2. Titanic (Steamship)—Juvenile literature. 3. Women
social reformers—United States—Biography—Juvenile literature. 4. Social reformers—United
States—Biography—Juvenile literature. 5. Denver (Colo.)—Biography—Juvenile. [1. Brown,
Margaret Tobin, 1867–1932 2. Reformers. 3. Women—Biography 4. Titanic (Steamship).] I. Title.
CT275.B7656 L36 2001   978.8'8303'092—dc21   [B]
00-057015

CRW 10 9 8 7 6 5 4 3

For Areilla Garmizo

Contents

Acknowledgments

MANY PEOPLE HELPED in researching this book. I'm grateful to the staff of the Western History/Genealogy Division of the Denver Public Library for finding newspaper articles that accurately reflected Margaret Brown's life and times, as well as for their assistance in providing important dates and links to other resources. The Colorado Historical Society, where the Brown family papers are kept, provided much valuable information. I am also indebted to Ruth Withers at the Missouri State Archives for supplying information on Margaret Brown's early life, and to Kathy Micklick of the Diocese of Colorado Springs for data on the Annunciation Church, where the Browns were married. Adrian Adams and Maureen Watry at the University of Liverpool in Liverpool, England, were indispensable in unearthing information on the *Titanic* tragedy. J. Hurley Hagood and Roberta Hagood graciously provided photographs from their private collection and Henry Sweets, Director of the Mark Twain Home Foundation, was key in providing photos and data on Mark Twain. Special thanks go to Elizabeth Walker, Curator, at the Molly Brown House Museum, who always went out of her way to find facts and answer questions.

Heroine of the *Titanic*

CHAPTER 1

"Water, Water, Water"

THE YEAR WAS 1911. The place, Cairo, Egypt. A forty-four-year-old American woman touring the country with her daughter and some friends had made her way through the twisted alleys of a crowded bazaar to a palm reader's parlor. She was curious to learn what the future held for her. But as the fortuneteller carefully studied the woman's palm, a look of misgiving slowly spread across his face. He shook his head, solemnly repeating the words, "Water, water, water."[1] In his limited English, the palmist added that he saw a sinking ship surrounded by drowning people.

The woman was not impressed with the reading and didn't hesitate to say so. She was aware that the fortuneteller knew she was a vacationing American who would eventually be going home on an ocean liner, and she thought no more about the experience. But perhaps the palm reader did have a premonition. The American tourist was Margaret Brown, and the ocean liner she would board to return to the United States was the ill-fated luxury ship the *Titanic*.

You may have heard of "the Unsinkable Molly Brown," the name the press gave Margaret. In 1912, as the "unsinkable" ship *Titanic* sank,

A seasoned traveler, Margaret Brown stayed at some of the world's most fashionable resorts. Here she poses on a sidewalk somewhere in Europe in 1928. *(The Denver Public Library, Western History Collection)*

she displayed courage and compassion when many of those in charge failed to do so. She became known as "the Unsinkable Mrs. Brown" and, later, as "the Unsinkable Molly Brown" and was the subject of a Broadway musical and a major motion picture.

Yet Margaret Brown was never called Molly during her lifetime, and much of what you think you know about her may be untrue. This is the story of who she really was and what really happened.

In 1912, Margaret Brown was an affluent, well-traveled woman whose frequent trips abroad took her to many parts of the world. She had recently toured Egypt with tycoon John Jacob Astor and his second wife, Madeleine. Astor had caused quite a scandal in New York by leaving the woman to whom he had been married for over ten years to be with Madeleine. While many people had nothing kind to say about the newlyweds, the couple found a sympathetic friend in Mrs. Brown. Also along on the trip was Margaret's twenty-two-year-old daughter, Helen.

After winding up their Egyptian visit, the touring Americans went to France. Margaret was looking forward to returning to the States in a few months. Summer was approaching, and as always she would spend it at the spacious house she rented in the fashionable resort of Newport, Rhode Island.

But while in Paris with Helen, Margaret received some unsettling news from home. Her son, Lawrence, sent word asking her to return immediately, as his young son, Lawrence Palmer Jr., was ill. Although Margaret carried the baby's picture with her, she had not actually seen the child yet. She was especially concerned because Larry, as her son was called, was not with the boy at the time. He had taken a ranching job in Oregon while his wife, Eileen, cared for the child at her mother's home in Kansas City.

Hoping to be of help, Margaret cut short her time abroad and booked passage on the next available vessel leaving for the United States. It was the *Titanic*. At first, her daughter was going to sail with her, but after her friends in Paris begged her to stay on, the young woman postponed her return.

Although Margaret had not planned to sail on the *Titanic*, she looked forward to being on the maiden voyage of the most luxurious ocean liner of its time. As she booked her passage, she never imagined that the voyage would change her life forever. Neither did any of the other passengers. In fact, the appeal of traveling on the *Titanic* was so strong that a number of first-class passengers switched their bookings from other ships in order to sail on it.

The first-class passenger list on the *Titanic* read like a society who's who. Nearly a dozen of the men on board had fortunes of over three hundred million dollars each. These included John Jacob Astor, with whom Margaret had recently toured Egypt. Also on the *Titanic* were banking and finance magnate Benjamin Guggenheim and Charles Hays, president of the Grand Trunk Railway. Other socially prominent passengers included Isidor Straus, presidential adviser and part owner of Macy's, Pennsylvania Railroad president John B. Thayer, and Broadway producer Henry B. Harris.

What attracted many of the prestigious ticket holders was the ship's splendor. On the nine-hundred-foot-long *Titanic*, the rich and famous could travel in the same style in which they lived. The magazine *The Shipbuilder* described the first-class accommodations as being "of unrivaled extent and magnificence." It further noted:

It took over two years to build the *Titanic,* at the time the largest vessel that had ever been constructed. The ship's length nearly equaled four city blocks.
(Library of Congress)

The first-class public rooms include the dining saloon, restaurant, lounge, reading and writing rooms, smoking room, and the veranda cafés and palm courts. Other novel features are the gymnasium, squash racquet court, Turkish and electric baths and the swimming bath. Magnificent suites of rooms, and cabins of size and style sufficiently diverse to suit the likes and dislikes of any passenger are provided. There is also a barber shop, a dark room for photographers, a clothes pressing room, a special dining room for maids and valets, a lending library, a telephone system, and a wireless telegraphy installation. Indeed everything has been done to make the first-class accommodations more than equal to that provided by the finest hotels on shore.[2]

Yet for all its amenities, the *Titanic* did not have enough lifeboats for everyone on board. The British White Star Line, which owned the *Titanic,* didn't see the need for them. The ship, which cost millions of dollars to build, was advertised as "the world's safest ocean liner" and was considered nearly hazard-free. It was equipped with wireless radios, and its hull was divided into separate watertight compartments. Of course, if several of these compartments were ripped open or otherwise destroyed at once, it was possible that the ship would sink. However, the White Star Line felt that that was too unlikely to consider seriously. Indeed, the company dispensed with the customary lifeboat drill usually given at a voyage's start.

Margaret Brown had sailed with the ship's captain, Edward J. Smith, on two other voyages and had once dined with him at the captain's table. She wasn't privy to some of the more unnerving rumors about this trip, but she probably heard talk of the White Star Line's hoping to break the speed record for crossing the Atlantic. This was Captain Smith's last trip for the line. After a lengthy career at sea, he was about to retire. Undoubtedly, attaining the fastest speed for a transatlantic crossing would be a wonderful climax to a distinguished career. With this in mind, the captain increased the vessel's speed daily.

At first, things went fairly well. Margaret knew quite a few of the other first-class passengers and enjoyed being with them. Mornings she rose early for an invigorating walk on the deck. Hoping to shed a few pounds on the voyage, she spent some time in the gymnasium. There she made good use of the stationary bike and punching bag.

Captain Edward Smith was born in England, the son of a potter. He was so popular among first-class passengers that he was often called the Millionaire's Captain. (*Library of Congress*)

At the time, boxing had become a fashionable form of exercise for women wishing to firm up their torso and arms. Mrs. Brown had even installed a leather punching bag in the renovated carriage house of her Denver, Colorado, home.

Neither she nor any of the other passengers had any idea that Captain Smith had already been notified of several iceberg sightings by other vessels, or that at noon on April 14 the following message had come over the *Titanic's* wireless radio: "Greek steamer *Athenai* reports passing icebergs and large quantities of field ice today." That evening at 9:30 P.M., the ship *Meshaba* delivered a similar warning when it radioed: "Much heavy pack ice and a great number of large icebergs ahead."[3]

Smith, however, did not slow the ship or add extra crew members to the watch that night. In the evening, Margaret dined with some friends, after which they relaxed in the ship's Palm Court, where a band played ragtime tunes. As it was especially chilly, many of the women

The Palm Court, complete with potted palms and wicker furniture, had a tropical flavor. The room's finishing touches were assembled just a week before the *Titanic* set sail. *(Library of Congress)*

wore fur coats over their evening gowns and savored the piping-hot coffee served from elegant silver pots. Later, in her cozy stateroom, Margaret put on a warm fleece nightgown before curling up in bed with a book she was anxious to finish.

It wasn't until about 11:35 P.M. that a crew member spotted the iceberg directly in front of the vessel, but at that point there was little anyone could do. Seconds later the *Titanic* scraped against the iceberg.

Damage to the ship during that collision would cause it to break in two and sink within hours.

Like so many other passengers, Margaret was caught off guard. She later wrote of the incident:

> So completely absorbed in my reading, I gave little thought to the crash that struck at my window overhead and threw me to the floor. Picking myself up I proceeded to see what the steamer had struck. On emerging from the stateroom, I found many men in the gangway in their pajamas. . . . All seemed to be listening, thinking nothing serious had occurred, though realizing at the time that the engines had stopped immediately after the crash and the boat was at a standstill.[4]

Although Margaret was thrown from her bed, others on board hardly felt the impact and therefore didn't realize the gravity of the situation. This was especially true of first-class passengers whose cabins were farthest from the damage. Initially, even some ship personnel didn't understand the seriousness of the predicament. But by midnight, flooding in the crew's quarters had reached dangerous levels.

Hearing the continuing commotion in the halls, Mrs. Brown ventured out of her cabin a second time to try to learn more. "I again looked out," she recalled, "and I saw a man whose face was blanched, his eyes protruding, wearing the look of a haunted creature. He was gasping for breath, and in an undertone he gasped, 'Get your lifesaver.'"[5]

Shortly after midnight, the lifeboats were readied and the first distress signals sent up. Margaret knew that people would be exposed to the frosty night air, and she dressed accordingly. She hurriedly put on her warmest outfit, a black velvet two-piece suit. Over that she wore a long overcoat and a sable stole. To make certain her legs stayed warm, she put on seven pairs of woolen stockings. While this layered look might not have been very flattering, Margaret was a practical as well as stylish woman, and she knew what the situation required.

She stuffed five hundred dollars in bills into her wallet and then took one last look around her stateroom. She realized that if they had to abandon the ship, she would be leaving all her possessions behind. She wondered if she would ever have a chance to finish the book she had been reading. Before going on deck she snatched a tiny turquoise figurine she had purchased in Egypt months before. Was she taking it for luck, or just as a keepsake from a memorable trip that now might end in the worst possible way? The reason didn't matter to her. She tucked it into her coat pocket and, after struggling to get on the bulky life jacket that hung in her room, headed for the boat deck.

Outside she soon found many who were far less well prepared. A number of men were still in pajamas, while some women stood shivering in their kimonos. Yet since the band was playing, Margaret, like many others, reasoned that things couldn't be all that bad. It wasn't known until later that the musicians had continued to play in order to keep the passengers calm.

Even as the ship's officers urged people to get into the lifeboats, some passengers were against abandoning ship. When Mrs. Brown met the Astors on deck, Mr. Astor indicated that he thought it foolish to leave such a massive ship for such a flimsy lifeboat. "Everything will be all right," he assured her.[6]

Quite a few first-class passengers pushed their way into the purser's office to retrieve the cash and jewels they had left there for safe-

John Jacob Astor and his new bride, Madeleine. *(Library of Congress)*

keeping. Although the purser's station was shut down and the passengers were told to put on their life jackets and immediately proceed to the lifeboat deck, some refused to do so. Instead, they stood their ground, arguing with the ship's staff and even threatening to sue the White Star Line.

While waiting on deck, Margaret talked with passengers, comforting several who seemed particularly upset. After noticing a group of women standing alone at one of the ship's bulkheads, she led them to where the lifeboats were lowered. After the crash, Mrs. Brown told the *Denver Post* in describing the mood aboard the ship:

I was busy at the moment trying to comfort a French woman, Mme. De Valler, who has now gone to Canada. She was of nobility. She came on the ship the smartest, most perfectly gowned woman I ever saw. She escaped in her nightdress, and she was frantic with fear. My heart ached for her.[7]

As the *Titanic* filled with water, the lifeboats began to fill with people. By then everyone had begun to take the captain's warnings seriously. The seating priority clearly reflected a class distinction: Third-class women and children were barred from the loading area until the women and children from first class were in the boats. John Jacob Astor assisted his wife as she stepped into Boat 4—the last lifeboat to leave the ship. He remained on board. Margaret, who had been helping to load Boat 6, never asked for a seat but nevertheless got one. "Suddenly I saw a shadow," she remembered, "and a few seconds later, I was taken hold of, and with the words 'You are going too,' was dropped fully four feet in the lowering lifeboat."[8] Like so many of the other lifeboats, Boat 6 was filled to less than half its capacity.

Three men and a number of other women were in the boat with Margaret. Quartermaster Robert Hitchens was supposed to take charge, but he never rose to the task. As soon as the lifeboat hit the water, he stood at the tiller announcing that the situation was hopeless. In a frightened voice, he said that it was futile to try to row away from the *Titanic* as it sank, since the suction from the huge ship would pull down everything for miles around. But a number of the women refused to believe him and, after picking up the oars from the bottom of the lifeboat, took turns rowing.

Seeing the *Titanic* go down from where she sat was an image Margaret would never forget. She later wrote, "Suddenly, there was a rift in the water, the sea opened up and the surface foamed like giant arms that spread around the ship."[9]

The quartermaster, who continued to complain, was against going back to pick up survivors from the water, even though there was room for over forty more people. The others, however, overruled him, and when he tried to stop them, Margaret threatened to throw him overboard. "Be quiet," she added, addressing Hitchens as though he were an insolent child. "Keep it to yourself if you feel that way. For the sake of these women and children, be a man. We have a smooth sea and a fighting chance."[10]

Seeing that she was not easily intimidated, Hitchens backed off. The women in Boat 6 saved several people from an icy death in the freezing Atlantic. Margaret also realized that the women rowing over to the people in the water had the additional benefit of keeping themselves warm. To help the other passengers, she pulled off the extra pairs of stockings she was wearing and passed them out to the women most in need. She also wrapped her sable stole around the waist of one man who looked nearly frozen, and made certain to cover his exposed legs with the tails of the fur wrap.

The quartermaster remained pessimistic, but Margaret was among those who tried to convince the others that help was surely on its way. Then, just before dawn, one of the women thought she saw a streak of lightning in the sky. Hitchens disagreed and insisted that it was a falling star. To everyone's relief, he was mistaken again. It was actually the ocean liner *Carpathia* coming to their rescue.

As the *Titanic* passengers boarded the *Carpathia,* the ship's staff and

Here *Titanic* survivors prepare to board the *Carpathia*. Having seen the ship from a distance, some passengers in lifeboats burned green flares to identify their location. *(Library of Congress)*

passengers did all they could to make them comfortable. Margaret recalled:

> Catching hold of the one thick rope, we were hoisted up to where a dozen of the crew and officers and doctor were waiting. Stimulants were given to those who needed them, and hot coffee was provided to all the survivors. Everything was done for our comfort, the *Carpathia* passengers sharing their staterooms, clothes, toilet-articles, then retiring to the far corner of the ship, where their deck-chairs were placed, giving the lounge up completely to the survivors.[11]

The Modern Historic Records Association

RMS "Carpathia"
Cunard S.S. Co Ltd
At Sea
April 27th 1912

At 12.35 am (ship's time) April 15th. Monday, 1912, I was called by the 1st officer in company with marconi operator & informed that the White Star Line R.M.S. "Titanic" was sending out urgent distress signals by wireless, that she had struck ice & required immediate assistance also giving position of "Titanic" as Lat 41°46' N. long 50°14' W.

I immediately ordered the "Carpathia" turned round sent for the Chief Engineer, made out Course & found we were then S52°E (true, 58 miles from "Titanic", also sent wireless to "Titanic" saying we were coming to his assistance.

The "Carpathia" was then on a voyage from New York to Mediterranean ports, with passengers mail & cargo.

I gave Chief Engineer instructions to turn out another watch of stokers & to make all speed possible.

I then ordered all our boats prepared & swung out ready for lowering. Interviewed the head officials of each department giving them all instructions I considered necessary to meet any Emergency, & had all hands called.

The night was beautifully fine but cold.

At 2.40 am saw Green flare up half a point on port bow (White Star Line Cos Signal) taking this to be the ship I immediately had rockets fired in answer, having previously given orders to fire Rockets at 3 am & each quarter hour after.

A few minutes after seeing the flare up we saw our first ice berg (having to alter Course several times from then on until our arrival on scene of disaster) to avoid icebergs.

We kept good bearings of the flare up which was shown about every quarter of an hour or so & answered with rockets & also with Cunard Cos night signals (Roman Candles throwing out stars).

At 4 am stopped the ship & at 4.10 am got first boat alongside the ship with officer in charge.

By the time the first boat was cleared it was breaking day, we could then see we were surrounded by ice bergs large & small & later saw extensive field ice close to.

On the officer coming aboard he reported Titanic foundered

Captain Rostron's handwritten account of the *Carpathia*'s rescue efforts. Ironically, the *Carpathia* would also later sink, after being hit by torpedoes during World War I. *(Library of Congress)*

The horrific loss was almost too great to comprehend. When two women survivors standing on the *Carpathia*'s deck were offered coffee, they simply continued to stare out at the sea. Without looking away from the water, one blankly replied, "Go away. We've seen our husbands drown."[12] Of the more than two thousand two hundred people on the *Titanic,* only about seven hundred survived.

CHAPTER 2

A Hero Among Us

MARGARET BROWN HAD acted heroically in Boat 6, but her leadership in dealing with the *Titanic* disaster didn't stop there. She was also invaluable to the survivors who were rescued by the *Carpathia*. Most of them were women, since it had been "women and children first" in loading the lifeboats.

The affluent women in first class had to face the emotionally devastating loss of their husbands. But for the women in third class the tragedy had even greater repercussions. The majority of these women were foreigners who, along with their spouses and children, were on their way to America to build a better life. Most were unskilled and unable to speak English. The death of their husbands meant the loss of the family breadwinner and their only source of income in a strange place far from home. Many now felt certain that they and their children would starve instead of prosper in the land of opportunity of which they had dreamed.

Margaret had previously studied a number of languages both abroad and at various schools in New York City. Her knowledge of foreign languages now proved extremely useful. Whenever possible, she spoke

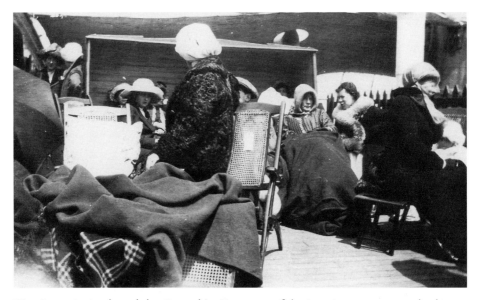

Titanic survivors aboard the *Carpathia*. For many of the immigrant women who lost their husbands, there would not be much more than the brief memorial service held on the ship for those who perished. *(Library of Congress)*

with these women at length, both to comfort them and to learn if any had friends or relatives in the United States who could take them in. In the days before the *Carpathia* reached New York, Margaret worked tirelessly, pledging her own money as well as wiring her wealthy friends to ask them to do the same for the destitute women.

She also urged wealthy *Titanic* survivors aboard the *Carpathia* to help, and she organized and chaired a committee on the rescue ship for this purpose. Although her friend Madeleine Astor was quite ill on the trip home, she did not hesitate to offer two thousand dollars for the cause.

Margaret Brown believed that all the women from the *Titanic* shared a special bond. "Sprinkled among the affluent," she noted,

The *Titanic* tragedy made headlines around the world. *(Library of Congress)*

"were our sisters of second class, and for a time there was that social leveling caused by the close proximity of death."[1] Yet she soon found that not everyone shared her sentiments.

When she asked several wealthy *Titanic* survivors to contribute to the relief fund, the women were uninterested. One, with a particularly puzzled look on her face, had answered, "Why, Mrs. Brown, why worry? I will be met by representatives of the Waldorf, who will take me at once to the hotel, and you, of course, will be greeted by the Ritz-Carlton, so why bother?"[2]

"But all these people will not have a Ritz-Carlton or Waldorf to receive them," Margaret retorted, finding it difficult to comprehend the woman's insensitivity.

The socialite's unfeeling response only spurred Margaret on to do more. Already known as an outstanding fundraiser in society circles, she put her skills to work aboard the *Carpathia*. She managed to secure between ten and fifteen thousand dollars for the needy before the ship even docked in New York.

Margaret was helpful on the *Carpathia* in different ways as well. A lounge on the ship was turned into a makeshift hospital, where she and others nursed ill survivors around the clock. She also made extensive lists of the names of survivors to be wired ashore from the ship. That way relatives of the *Titanic* passengers could learn as soon as possible if their loved ones were alive.

When the *Carpathia* arrived in New York, Margaret did not leave the ship with the other first-class passengers but remained on board for an extra day. She wanted to be certain that the immigrant women and children who had friends or family members meeting them were able to find one another. She wrote:

Feeling a duty to remain after the army of Red Cross doctors and nurses, White Star officials, and general Aid Corps [primarily the Travelers Aid Society] had taken leave of the ship, we found it was

Fueled by rumors, huge crowds gathered in front of the White Star Line's New York office on April 15, 1912, for news of the *Titanic.* Not knowing that the vessel was already at the bottom of the Atlantic Ocean, company vice president P.A.S. Franklin assured the crowds that the ship was "practically unsinkable." *(Library of Congress)*

necessary to improvise beds in the lounge, so I remained with them on board all night. There were many who had friends on the dock, but did not know them, so with each one was sent an escort and the names called out.[3]

Once the newcomers were matched up, Margaret provided the White Star Line agents with a list of these passengers' new addresses.

Word of Margaret Brown's bravery, heroism, and goodwill had preceded her to New York, and when she stepped off the ship, she was thronged by reporters. Both the press and politicians embraced her, and she became an instant national celebrity. Before long, there was talk of petitioning Congress to give her a medal, and many thought a statue should be erected in her honor.

Although the limelight was focused on her, Margaret never lost touch with the immigrant women on the *Titanic* who were now widows. From her hotel room in New York City she continued to ask others to see to their welfare. Referring to one woman from Russia who had lost her husband as well as her money and clothing on the *Titanic,* she said, "I would like to take this young Russian woman to Denver with me, but I've already got three adopted women."[4]

In addition, Margaret worked with the various consulates to find places for the immigrant survivors, even as she continued soliciting funds for them. She remained chairperson of the Survivors' Committee, which had been formed on the *Carpathia,* raising several thousand dollars to be distributed among the *Carpathia*'s crew members who had worked so diligently to assist the survivors. The committee further determined to do whatever it could to see that the White Star Line made adequate reparations to the families of those who had perished.

Captain Arthur H. Rostron of the *Carpathia* heartily praised Margaret Brown for the help she gave aboard his ship, and she, in turn, thought Rostron was a hero in his own right. In May she returned to New York from Denver to participate in a ceremony during which the Survivors' Committee presented the *Carpathia*'s captain with a silver

Margaret Brown posing with Captain Rostron, who is holding the silver loving cup presented to him by the Survivors' Committee. The trophy, symbolizing victory, was given to Rostron in recognition of his heroic actions. *(Library of Congress)*

loving cup. All *Carpathia* crew members were also awarded medals. Margaret had a special, more personal, gift for Rostron as well. She gave him the tiny Egyptian turquoise statue she had carried in her pocket throughout her ordeal at sea. She felt it had brought her luck and hoped it would do the same for the courageous and compassionate gentleman who had saved her and the other *Titanic* survivors. Touched by her thoughtfulness, the captain treasured the gift for years.

Margaret was among the women who raised funds for this *Titanic* memorial in Washington, D.C. Its inscription reads: TO THE BRAVE MEN WHO PERISHED IN THE WRECK OF THE TITANIC APRIL 15, 1912. THEY GAVE THEIR LIVES THAT WOMEN AND CHILDREN MIGHT BE SAVED. *(Library of Congress)*

However, Margaret had no kind words for the crew of the *Titanic*, whose unprofessional behavior, she felt, contributed to the tremendous loss of life. "Those women who perished were lost because they were not notified of the wreck," she told reporters in New York. "The stewards failed in their duty, they deserted. Aside from the first few officers, the crew was a lot of scrubs."[5]

Margaret Brown never forgot those who lost their lives on the *Titanic*. She often said that she didn't think of herself as a hero and only wished she could have done more. Fourteen years later, she visited a cemetery in Halifax, Nova Scotia, where many of the *Titanic* victims were buried. She came to lay wreaths that she had made on each of their graves.

CHAPTER 3

It Started in Hannibal

T HE *TITANIC* TRAGEDY marked a turning point in Margaret Brown's life. Ironically, her life had begun near the water, though in a far humbler setting. Margaret was born in the Mississippi River town of Hannibal, Missouri, on July 18, 1867. She was the daughter of Irish immigrants John and Johanna Tobin. Both her parents had been previously widowed, and each had a daughter from their first marriage. So in addition to her brothers, Daniel and William, and her sister, Helen, Margaret also grew up with two half sisters named Katie and Mary Ann.

Hannibal, which had a population of about twenty thousand people at the time, was a good place for the Tobins to be. It had a strong Irish Catholic community, and the family fit in well. The Tobins were proud of their Irish roots and took an active role in church and community activities. Being something of a tomboy, Margaret, who was often called Maggie, spent many afternoons exploring the haunts of Hannibal with her brother Daniel and his friends. Though Margaret especially liked being with Daniel and her younger sister, Helen, she was close to all her siblings and would remain so throughout her life.

The Tobin children attended Mary O'Leary's Prospect Avenue grammar school, which was run by Johanna Tobin's sister, the children's aunt. Margaret went there until she was thirteen and, contrary to early stage and screen portrayals of her, learned to read and write quite well. The school wasn't far from the Tobin home, which sat on a hill just blocks from the waterway.

The entire family lived in a small four-room wood dwelling that had only one bedroom. There was a cow, some chickens, and a vegetable garden on the property. While Margaret's early years were hardly filled with luxuries, she was never as poor as she was frequently portrayed. Her father dug ditches for the Hannibal Gas Works, one of the town's largest employers. The hours were long and the pay low, but he always kept a roof over their heads and food on the table. There were many homes in Hannibal like the Tobins', in which working-class children thrived before setting out to seek their own fortunes.

The Tobin household grew smaller as the children grew older and left to marry and start families of their own, or went out to work to help with the family's expenses. Margaret's half sister Katie married a man named John A. Becker from the Alsace-Lorraine region of France. The couple bought a home not far from the Tobins' and opened up a candy shop, which soon became a favorite stop among local schoolchildren.

Margaret spent a good deal of time at John and Katie's home as well as at their confectionery. Her brother-in-law was especially good with children, and Margaret enjoyed watching the young customers make their selections from the wide assortment of penny candy. For just a penny they could also leave with one of the delicious large sugar cookies Katie baked.

While the Beckers lived in Hannibal for the rest of their lives, that wasn't the case with Margaret's other half sister, Mary Ann, and her husband, Jack Landgrin. Jack was a young man with bigger dreams, though his hopes for the future were not unlike those of many young people in the 1880s. Jack wanted to go west to seek his fortune.

When gold was discovered in California and Colorado in the mid-1800s, thousands had headed west hoping to strike it rich. In some ways, the Gold Rush changed the meaning of success. Now even a poor person could become a millionaire—often overnight. One did not need the proper family background or education. Many new millionaires had no more than the courage to take to the road and the right amount of luck.

In 1877, silver was discovered in Leadville, Colorado, and as news of fast-made fortunes spread, another mineral rush began. Investors and miners from as far away as London set their sights on Leadville. As a skilled blacksmith, Jack Landgrin believed there would be more than ample work in the new boomtown, and he convinced his wife that he was right. It wasn't long before other members of the Tobin family felt the lure of the West as well. Margaret's brother Daniel, who worked selling newspapers at the railroad station in Hannibal, also believed the future in Leadville might be limitless.

So it wasn't a surprise when, in the autumn of 1883, Jack and Mary Ann Landgrin, along with Daniel Tobin, boarded a train bound for Leadville. Shortly after arriving, Jack began to build a blacksmith business, which was soon thriving. Mary Ann became pregnant with the first of the couple's eleven children. Daniel, who hoped to try mining, lived with Jack and Mary Ann at their East Fifth Street house for a time before getting a place of his own nearby.

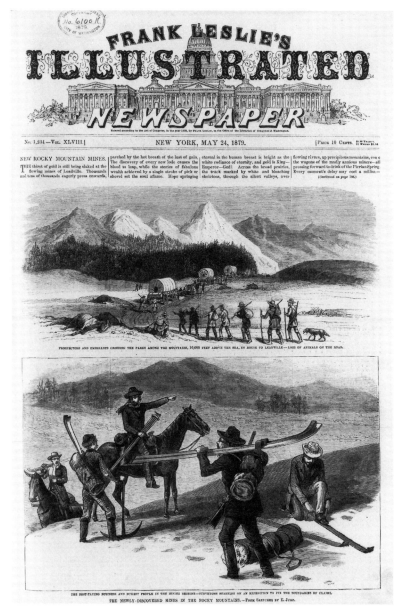

News of riches in the West excited everyone. In these illustrations, prospectors are making their way through the mountains, and surveyors are setting claim boundaries.
(Library of Congress)

The railroad station in Hannibal, Missouri, was the starting point for Margaret's journey west. (*J. Hurley Hagood and Roberta Hagood Collection*)

Three years later, in 1886, Daniel finally had enough money to purchase railway tickets to Leadville for his sisters, Margaret and Helen. Helen, who was just fifteen, would be staying for only a brief visit, but he hoped Margaret would remain.

Perhaps the only other person more excited than Daniel about the trip was Margaret herself. Though she liked Hannibal and was extremely close to her parents, there was little to keep her there. After completing grammar school, she worked in Garth's tobacco factory, where she spent long hours in a humid room stripping the leaves off tobacco plant stems. While the men at Garth's who were hired to roll cigars could make up to two dollars a day, girls like Margaret earned only a fraction of that, and there was no chance for advancement.

Margaret lived with her brother Daniel in Leadville until she married. Later, Daniel married and had four children. *(Colorado Historical Society)*

If Margaret Tobin had been a more typical girl, she might have remained in Hannibal and eventually married someone not unlike her father. But even at nineteen, it was clear that the young woman who was once a tomboy wanted more. She had heard of the fabulous fortunes made out west and was intrigued by the possibilities.

Nevertheless, leaving Hannibal to begin a new life was a daring move for any young woman. Everyone knew the phrase "Go west,

Female barbers in front of their shop. Notice the words painted on their front windows: Lady Barber • Haircutting • Shaving. *(The Denver Public Library, Western History Collection)*

young man," and as in the days of the Gold Rush the majority of those going west were just that—young men. Far fewer women made the journey, and most of those who did were either wives, like Margaret's half sister Mary Ann, or prostitutes.

But Margaret was willing to take a chance. She had no intention of buying a pick and ax and becoming a prospector, yet she felt certain that her life would be enhanced in Leadville. There were so many more opportunities in this still-unsettled territory—even for women.

Margaret knew that sometimes women found work in businesses that had been set up to provide the goods and services miners needed to build new towns and lives. Others managed boardinghouses or took in laundry for the miners.

Margaret wanted more for both herself and her parents, especially her father, who she felt had always done his best for their family. She later commented:

> I longed to be rich enough to give him a home so that he would not have to work. I used to think that the zenith of happiness would be to have my father come to his home after a pleasant day and find his slippers warmed and waiting for him. It was a little thing to want, I thought. Of course, we could have had his slippers ready for him in those days, you will say, but Father was too tired when his work was done to enjoy any comfort. His life was bounded by working and sleeping.[1]

Although no one would have guessed it, Margaret's trip west would change her—and her parents'—lives in ways she had never imagined possible.

There are many stories about Margaret's life. Some are true, some are half true, and others are completely untrue. One story has her meeting the famous American author Mark Twain (Samuel Clemens) while waitressing in Hannibal's Park Hotel before she left Missouri. Margaret supposedly struck up a conversation with Clemens, who encouraged her to try her luck in the West.

Is the story true or false? Hannibal was the writer's boyhood home, and he often returned there in later life. However, it is not known if

Mark Twain was born in Florida, but his family moved to Hannibal when he was four years old. He and Margaret are probably the town's best-known residents. *(Mark Twain Museum)*

Mark Twain ever stayed at the Park Hotel—or if Margaret worked there, for that matter. Mark Twain did indeed visit Hannibal just months before Margaret's departure, but it is not certain if their paths ever crossed or if he influenced her decision to go to Leadville.

CHAPTER 4

Life in Leadville

W HEN MARGARET ARRIVED in Leadville, it was still something of a rip-roaring boomtown. Filled with people hoping to get rich quick, it was nothing like her hometown of Hannibal. Leadville had 120 saloons and 118 gambling houses, with some of these establishments remaining open for business twenty-four hours a day. There was also no shortage of con artists, and prostitutes were readily available to anyone who could pay the price.

Once the large Leadville mining companies had installed telephones in 1878 to facilitate their business transactions, only male operators were hired—the rough language used in the conversations was not considered proper for a young lady's ears. There were other unusual twists in bringing basic services to Leadville. To protect the town's many hastily built wood structures, volunteer fire companies were organized. However, they had to be disbanded in favor of salaried firefighters after an investigation revealed that during a blaze a group of "intoxicated firemen did steal . . . [from the saloon of William Roberts] 600 cigars and a lot of liquor and beer."[1]

Yet it was clear that, almost simultaneously, culture had begun to

Like other establishments of its kind, this Leadville saloon did not lack for patrons. Its varied décor included a coat rack made of deer hooves, mounted animal heads, a music box, and gaming machines. *(The Denver Public Library, Western History Collection)*

take root in the mining town. A free reading room—the closest thing Leadville had to a public library—opened and proved to be quite popular among the townspeople. The Tabor Opera House, which featured a wide array of talent, was also established, as was the Twin Lakes Lodge, a fashionable resort that catered to potential mining investors from the East and abroad.

Religion and charity were not overlooked, either. The Annunciation Church, where Margaret worshiped, was built in 1879 after the

Sacred Heart, Leadville's first Catholic church, could no longer accommodate the growing number of parishioners. Under the church's auspices, a local hospital and orphanage were soon established.

Margaret felt at home in Leadville's substantial Irish Catholic community. Following the lead of her half sister and brother-in-law, she participated in church activities and frequently attended church-sponsored picnics, socials, and various other functions. Although she missed her parents and siblings back home, she never regretted her decision to move to Leadville, and she returned there to visit throughout her life. The bustling new mining town had an air of excitement and promise that appealed to her.

But that didn't mean that at first life in Leadville was easy for either her or her brother, with whom she lived. Daniel worked in the mines nearly twelve hours a day and earned less than fifty dollars a month. He dreamed of becoming rich as a miner, but by 1886 such lucky strikes had become increasingly rare. With much of the surface ore gone, large mining corporations in the East now dominated the industry. Equipped with sufficient capital and machinery to launch large-scale mining operations, these concerns employed many would-be independent miners. Despite his hopes to the contrary, Daniel Tobin was among them.

Margaret didn't look for work immediately. There was a lot to do in helping Daniel set up a household. Margaret added a feminine touch to the house they rented by sewing curtains and tablecloths for the kitchen and arranging what furniture they had. She hoped to enhance her brother's life by both her company and her cooking.

Before long, though, Margaret realized that she would have to earn some money. Living in Leadville was costly, and it was hard for them to get by on just Daniel's salary. A sack of flour cost nearly four dollars, and meat and rent were expensive, too.

Fortunately, Margaret's search for employment turned out surprisingly well for a single girl in a rough-and-tumble mining town. While she did not become an independent businesswoman, she managed to avoid the typical pitfalls common to unmarried women venturing west. Margaret never cleaned houses or worked in one of the many saloons. Instead, she found steady employment sewing carpets and drapes at the Daniels, Fisher & Smith dry goods store on Harrison Avenue.

Margaret's excellent sewing skills made her a valuable addition to the staff, and she was well liked by both her coworkers and supervisors. Years later, her coworker Thomas E. Cahill described her flatteringly in a letter to her son. "She was a very capable and pleasant employee," he wrote, "and all her fellow employees were very fond of her. . . . She was exceptionally bright, a most interesting conversationalist, had a charming personality and this coupled with her beauty made her a very attractive woman."[2]

Though Margaret's quick wit and vivaciousness were refreshing, some might disagree with Cahill's description of her as beautiful. Her cousin Lorraine Schuck felt that Margaret's attractiveness was most apparent in the way she carried herself. "She always stood very upright," the young woman noted, "and there was something very regal about her."[3] Her thick curly hair, pretty blue eyes, and lovely complexion also added to her appeal.

It wasn't long before Margaret caught the eye of James Joseph Brown at a church picnic. J. J., as he was called, was a handsome mining engineer from Wymert, Pennsylvania, who thought that Margaret

A view of Leadville when it was a bustling western boomtown. By 1880 it already had thousands of residents. *(Colorado Historical Society)*

would make an excellent wife. At the time, marriage was an important option for women. It was one of the few ways a woman could financially improve her lot, since females were unofficially barred from most lucrative types of employment.

By going west, Margaret had escaped the drudgery of stripping tobacco stems, but she still didn't make a high salary. It is likely that despite her sewing skills she earned only a fraction of what her brother made. Even though that was more than she had earned in Hannibal, it cost considerably more to live in Leadville. After assessing the situation, Margaret set her sights on finding a rich husband, which would

A young Margaret wearing a pearl choker with a cross pendant. Margaret's religious faith remained strong throughout her lifetime. *(The Denver Public Library, Western History Collection)*

42

enable her to help her parents as well as improve her own lifestyle. But if that's what she was looking for, James Joseph Brown did not fit her image.

Like Margaret, J.J. Brown was the offspring of Catholic parents who had immigrated to the United States from Ireland. James Joseph's mother, Cecilia Palmer, was a schoolteacher who had stressed the importance of learning to her son throughout his childhood. To her delight, J.J. proved to be a good student and an avid reader.

In 1877, James Joseph Brown left his family's home in Pennsylvania to pursue a mining career. He was smarter than many miners. He knew that with most of the surface ore gone, a miner needed a well-thought-out mining plan based on an accurate picture of the area's landscape. So while working for a mining company during the day, he studied geology at night.

J.J. also explored different mining techniques and their variations, devising unique approaches to the more challenging problems. Before long, it was generally agreed that he had "gained a special genius for practical and economic geology."[4] As might be expected, he rose to a management position and eventually ran a fairly large mine.

J.J. Brown was a miner with an exceptional mind. And in the summer of 1886, Margaret Tobin was on his mind. At first, it did not look as though the feeling was mutual. While J.J. was immediately taken with Margaret, initially she seemed uninterested in him and practically ignored his advances. Although both J.J. and Margaret were Irish Catholics, there was quite an age difference between the two. J.J. was thirty-one years old when he met nineteen-year-old Margaret, and in the beginning she thought of him as an "old man." But Brown was captivated by the young woman's contagious laugh and boundless energy and was not easily discouraged. He began courting her, which included taking her for horse-and-buggy drives in the countryside on Sunday afternoons.

Margaret was her usual outspoken self around J.J. On what was to be their first outing, he supposedly called for her in a shabby-looking rig. Margaret is said to have stood in the doorway and exclaimed, "You're not taking me out in that!" Another man might have left and not come back, but J.J. took the insult in stride and remedied the situation. According to the story, the following week he showed up in a brand-new horse-drawn carriage.

Before long, the two began seeing quite a bit of each other. Both Margaret and J.J. liked to dance, and they made a fine couple on the dance floor at church socials. As Thomas Cahill reported, "It was easy to see that at about this time the handsome young Jim Brown fell in love with her. . . . Everybody in Leadville thought it a wonderful match."[5]

As the weeks passed, the relationship grew less one-sided. Margaret found herself anxious to see more of J.J. Together they enjoyed evenings at the Tabor Opera House, dining out, long walks, playing cards, and being with the many friends both of them had in Leadville. In many ways, James Joseph seemed perfect for her, but there was still one stumbling block nineteen-year-old Margaret needed to get past.

While J.J. did well at his job, he certainly was not wealthy, and Margaret felt that if she married him, she would never be able to make her father comfortable in his old age. She later said of her predicament:

I wanted a rich man, but I loved Jim Brown. I thought about how I wanted comfort for my father and how I had determined to stay

An amateur theatrical group poses for a picture inside the Tabor Opera House, where Margaret and J.J. enjoyed productions while courting. *(The Denver Public Library, Western History Collection)*

single until a man presented himself who could give to the tired old man the things I longed for him. Jim was as poor as we were, and had no better chance in life. I struggled hard with myself in those days. I loved him, but he was poor.[6]

Perhaps it was J.J.'s persistence that finally won Margaret. James Joseph pursued her with the same fervor he put into mining. "Finally I decided that I'd be better off with a poor man whom I loved than

Margaret's father, John Tobin, shared his daughter's concern for others. After coming to this country from Ireland, he became active in the abolitionist movement to free the slaves. *(Hannibal Free Public Library)*

with a wealthy one whose money had attracted me," she said, looking back on her reasons. "So I married Jim Brown. I gave up cooking for my brother and moved to Jim's cabin."[7]

The couple were wed on September 1, 1886, at the Annunciation Church. At the time, Margaret had been in town less than a year, but she felt certain that she wanted to spend the rest of her life with the man she was marrying. Being smart, energetic, and in love, Margaret hoped she and J.J. could make all the right things happen for them. The service was performed by Father Henry Robinson, and most of Margaret's family from Hannibal were there for the occasion.

Margaret's bridesmaid was Margaret Boylan, a housemaid who was also a close friend, while J.J.'s best man was a local barber named Thomas Greeley. Gifts to the newlyweds included a solid silver tea

Twin Lakes, south of Leadville in Lake County, where Margaret and J.J. honeymooned. *(The Denver Public Library, Western History Collection)*

set from the men at the mine where J.J. worked. After the ceremony there was a wedding breakfast for the couple at the Evergreen Lakes Hotel near Leadville, and Margaret and J.J. honeymooned at the Twin Lakes resort.

Margaret and J.J. were a popular couple in Leadville, and their marriage was duly noted by the society editor of the Leadville paper, the *Herald Democrat*. He wrote:

> A wedding which attracted considerable attention took place at the Church of the Annunciation at two o'clock in the afternoon. The contracting parties were James J. Brown, the popular superintendent of the Louisville mine, and Miss Maggie Tobin, the accomplished young saleslady [Margaret also sewed there] from whom the patrons of Daniels, Fisher & Smith will invoke the richest blessings.[8]

Although the new Mrs. Brown didn't know it, her girlhood dreams were about to come true. The man she married for love would soon become one of the wealthiest miners in America.

CHAPTER 5

The Newlyweds

AFTER THE HONEYMOON, Margaret quickly settled into her new role as homemaker. The newlyweds lived in J. J.'s two-room cabin just outside of Leadville in the small community of Stumptown. There were a number of places like Stumptown in the area. Located close to the mines, these mini-mining towns enabled miners to get to work regardless of heavy winter sleet and snow.

Stumptown made Leadville look luxurious. It had no sidewalks— just a single dirt road leading into and out of it. The houses and cabins were mostly small, and none had indoor plumbing. Instead, Stumptown residents used outhouses and drew their water for cooking and bathing from the town pump.

Most Stumptown families depended on wood-burning stoves to survive the region's brutal winters, and it was during this season that there was a story about the Browns' fortune burning up in their stove. According to this famous but untrue tale, after making a rich strike, J. J. handed Margaret a sack of paper money and told her to hide it in the house. Since the weather was unseasonably warm, she put the bag in the wood-burning stove, which had not been used for months.

A view of Stumptown, overlooking Mosquito Pass. Margaret's cabin there would be the humblest of her homes as a married woman. *(The Denver Public Library, Western History Collection)*

Margaret went to bed early that evening, while J. J. went out to celebrate with some men from the mine.

When he returned later that night, there was a chill in the air. Not knowing that the money was in the stove, J. J. lit a fire. The next morning when Margaret saw what had happened, she is said to have cried hysterically. J. J. supposedly quickly comforted her, saying,

"Never mind, darling, I'll make that much again for you—and more!"[1] Early reports had J.J. burning about ten thousand dollars, but as the story was repeated, the amounts cited were sometimes as high as three hundred thousand dollars.

In reality, paper money wasn't in use in the area until after World War I. Yet there was a grain of truth to the story. Margaret actually hid about seventy-five dollars in gold and silver coins in the stove, but it was from J.J.'s company's petty cash box, which he had brought home that weekend for safekeeping. After the fire died out, the couple sifted through the ashes and recovered the coins. Years later when Margaret told the story, she ended it by saying, "Suppose it had been paper money."[2]

While Stumptown had fewer conveniences than Leadville, the Browns liked it well enough, and both of them made some lifelong friends there. After marrying J.J., Margaret grew determined to become better educated. Since J.J. earned more than most mine-workers, she was able to pay teachers in Leadville to tutor her in literature, art, and music. The Browns also hired a young girl from Ireland named Mary A. Fitzharris Nevin to help with the housework and cooking. Margaret enjoyed Mary's company, and the two young women frequently attended Margaret's tutoring sessions together.

Though Stumptown was closer to J.J.'s job, after about a year the Browns moved into a larger home in Leadville. The family was growing. Margaret had become pregnant shortly after the couple married, and on August 30, 1887, their son, Lawrence Palmer Brown, was born. They gave the child his middle name to honor J.J.'s mother, Cecilia Palmer. Margaret went back to Hannibal to have the baby so that she could be with her family.

Before long, the Browns moved from their Ninth Street house to a still bigger Leadville home on West Seventh Street. This house was ideal for many reasons. Besides having several bedrooms and a large kitchen, it was just blocks away from both Margaret's brother Daniel and her half sister. The siblings and their spouses frequently visited one another and shared many happy holiday celebrations. When the rest of the family came out from Hannibal to see them, it almost felt like old times.

Margaret and J.J. were active in community social events. They enjoyed church functions, winter sleighing parties, and the popular costume balls in town. When Margaret became pregnant again, she didn't need to go back to Hannibal to have the baby. By then, most of her family had joined her in Leadville. Margaret's parents came along with her nineteen-year-old brother, William, and her seventeen-year-old sister, Helen. J.J. got her father a night watchman's job at the mine he ran, and her brother found work in a local cigar-making factory. J.J.'s brother Edward and his sister Helen soon came to Leadville as well.

Margaret had her family nearby when she gave birth to her second child on July 1, 1889. This time it was a girl, and though the child was named Catherine Ellen, everyone called her Helen. Later, in looking back on her life, Margaret would say that these were her happiest years.

Her days were not completely taken up with family life and social functions, however. She was also active in charitable causes. Unlike most women of her time, she did more than merely help out with church bake sales or fold bandages at the local hospital. She was extremely concerned with bringing quality education to Leadville and often spoke out on this matter.

But perhaps the cause nearest to her heart was the fight for miners'

Margaret and J.J. pose with their two young children in a photographer's studio.
(Colorado Historical Society)

A miner and his family on the porch of their cabin. Mining families enjoyed few comforts and almost no company benefits. *(The Denver Public Library, Western History Collection)*

rights and the welfare of their families. She saw how many mining company owners and executives fared well while the men who worked the mines often barely made ends meet. Miners were routinely subjected to dangerous conditions and health hazards on the job, and when a miner died or became disabled, his family was usually left destitute.

Margaret did her best to help these mining families in any way she could. She ran soup kitchens, sponsored clothing drives, and sought ways to better educate the children. If she had no one with whom to leave her own children when she met with miners' wives, she took them with her. Before long, she earned a reputation as someone who could get the job done. Though she was still a young woman, it was obvious that she cared about social injustice and wanted to see more humane conditions instituted in mining.

Nevertheless, the fact that she was a woman hampered her efforts. It was difficult for a female to be taken seriously and to effect meaningful societal reforms when women didn't even have the right to vote yet. Margaret was also the wife of someone who managed mines and was on his way up in the industry. As a loyal company man, J.J. tended to put profits ahead of employee benefits on his scale of priorities.

This became particularly evident after Margaret learned that large numbers of miners were dying from silicosis, a condition resulting from dust buildup in their lungs. J.J. felt that the mining companies were not responsible, but his wife saw things differently. In time, the basic philosophical differences between Margaret and her husband would deepen and cause a rift in their relationship. While the Browns still lived in Leadville, however, outside events had an even greater impact on their lives.

By 1892, Leadville's boom period was ending. The price of silver sharply dropped as the many new mines dramatically increased the metal's availability. The predicament worsened in 1893 when the Sherman Silver Purchase Act was repealed, making gold the only metal backing U.S. currency. Widespread unemployment soon characterized the once thriving town of Leadville, which some felt now might be more aptly called "Deadville."

The Browns were among the fortunate ones who survived the industry's downward spiral. In 1891, J.J. had purchased a sizable

During the 1880s boardinghouses for miners like this one overflowed with men. A decade later, a financial panic caused silver mines to close, banks to fail, and boardinghouses to become vacant. *(The Denver Public Library, Western History Collection)*

amount of stock in the Ibex Mining Company. Ibex had previously extracted large quantities of lead and silver from a high-producing mine in the area known as the Little Jonny. Since the mine had also yielded some gold and high-quality copper at one time, in 1893 Ibex decided to actively mine it for gold. It was a fairly perilous endeavor, as there were continual cave-ins at the site, which jeopardized both worker safety and the operation's profitability.

J.J., however, was unusually resourceful in devising measures to overcome the various obstacles. He even quit his job at the mine where he'd been working to devote all his time and attention to the

"LITTLe Jhonny" WoRLds Richest gold mine
At LeadvilIe, Colo.

The Little Jonny Mine made J.J. Brown both rich and famous. Newspapers throughout America reported his success. *(Colorado Historical Society)*

Little Jonny. Eventually, the Little Jonny yielded far more gold than the Ibex Company stockholders had ever imagined possible. As a major shareowner, J.J. suddenly became extremely wealthy. Amazingly, the Brown family fortune was made in gold in a silver town that was going bust.

CHAPTER 6

Onward to Denver

THE BROWNS DIDN'T remain in Leadville very long after making their fortune. By 1894, the family, including Margaret's parents, had moved to the more prestigious city of Denver. Margaret did not forget those she left behind in Leadville, however, and besides giving them all the furnishings from her Leadville home, she often visited.

In Denver, Maggie and J.J. purchased a graceful Victorian home at 1340 Pennsylvania Avenue, in the city's fashionable Capitol Hill section. Their new house was only about three blocks from the state capitol, and while it was not as large as some Denver homes, the Browns' residence had three stories and a total area of 7,719 square feet.

The parlors, library, kitchen, and dining room were on the first floor; the bedrooms, study, sunroom, and bath took up the second; and the servants' quarters were on the third, or top, level of the house. The Brown home was later sometimes called the House of the Lions because of the carved lions in both sitting and standing positions that were eventually placed at the front entrance. Although the original owner had paid between fifteen thousand and eighteen thousand dollars, the Browns bought the house for thirty thousand dollars.

Margaret made a number of changes to their Denver home's exterior. These included having a stone wall built in front of the residence. *(The Denver Public Library, Western History Collection)*

It didn't take Margaret long to become involved in Denver's social and political scene. She had tremendous drive and now channeled all her energy into these activities. As always, her outlets were limited by the customs of the times. In the late 1890s, wealthy women didn't control large companies or run for political office. Instead, they were often expected to be elegant hostesses who entertained lavishly, both socially and for charitable causes. Margaret approached the task with style and flair. She even managed to stretch the role somewhat, proving that she was a true trailblazer.

From the moment she set foot in Denver, she left nothing to chance. She furnished her home with elaborate and expensive items from around the world. The things she chose reflected a number of

John and Johanna Tobin enjoyed their days at their daughter's Denver home. The Brown children would fondly remember the wonderful stories their grandfather told. *(Colorado Historical Society)*

different decorating styles. Special touches from her early days in the West included the coyote heads hung in the front hall. There was also a genuine polar bear rug in the parlor.

When the Browns switched to hot-water heating, Margaret had gold-painted radiators decorated with cupids and small fish installed throughout the house. "Maggie always had the latest," a museum curator would later say of her taste. "If the platform rocker came in, she had it. If wicker furniture came in, she had that."[1]

Shortly after purchasing their home, the Browns enlarged the carriage house accompanying it. They kept their carriage and harnesses in the original part of the building and built additional stalls and a hayloft for the horses. A living area on the second floor was created for their stable boy. While the horse-drawn carriage was the basic mode of transportation at the time, Margaret also liked to ride. In addition, the Brown children had their own small carriage, which was pulled by their pony.

Lawrence and Helen were sent to the best schools, and Margaret sought to enhance her own education as well. "Perhaps no woman in society has ever spent more time or money becoming 'civilized' than Mrs. Brown," the *Denver Times* wrote of her.[2] While living in Denver, she traveled to New York City for several months to study drama, music, and literature. She also took up foreign languages and frequently traveled to Europe to heighten her awareness of the cultural scene abroad.

While in France, she worked intensively on her language skills with a well-known teacher. She later recalled:

I'll never forget the first time I went to him. He pulled a cork from a champagne bottle and ordered me to put it in my mouth — the cork, not the bottle. "That will make you hold your mouth open when you talk," he informed me and didn't even smile when I told him I thought most people preferred me with it shut.[3]

Margaret's ongoing quest for self-improvement did not go unnoticed in the society pages. "It has always been to [Margaret's] credit," commented one paper, "that she realized that social leadership

The Brown children enjoyed rides in their pony cart. Here, their mother keeps a watchful eye on them from the porch. *(Colorado Historical Society)*

required something more than the ability to pay a good chef and the taste to select a clever dressmaker."[4]

Yet Margaret Brown was also known to pay careful attention to fashion, and she put a tremendous amount of work into building her fantastic wardrobe. She had gowns and traveling clothes, along with hats and shoes to match, for every occasion. Many of her outfits came from Paris designers, and were made out of rich brocades, taffeta, and fine silks. She worked closely with her dressmakers to find the most figure-flattering styles, and she also tried not to be seen in public in the same outfit twice.

Local society editors soon realized that Mrs. Brown was likely to be the most spectacularly dressed woman at an event, and they noted this in their columns. After seeing a photograph of her at the opera one evening, a columnist wrote: "That fabulous gilt lace gown of hers was described in the Parisian press as one of the most elaborate gowns ever created. . . . Three months were consumed in weaving the lace, and then, after the lace [was sewn] it was spangled and embroidered in gold."[5]

Margaret did not skimp on jewelry, either. She liked the sparkle of diamonds and owned diamond pendants, bracelets, and rings. Some of her solid gold hair clips were decorated with diamonds and other precious gems as well.

Once, at a luncheon, a friend of Margaret's pointed out another woman, noting that it "wasn't proper to wear diamonds in the daytime." Margaret, who both followed and dictated fashion, is said to have answered, "I didn't think so either until I had some!"[6] A thief who broke into the Browns' residence was reportedly caught with over forty thousand dollars' worth of jewelry—a remarkable amount, especially considering that the Browns' stylish home cost only thirty thousand. It's clear that Margaret enjoyed wearing expensive gems.

The Broadway and early Hollywood versions of Margaret's life portrayed her giving parties to which no one came, but that was hardly the case. The Browns were part of Denver society and as early as 1894 were regularly listed in Denver's social directory. Margaret was a member of the Denver Women's Club and the Denver Women's Press Club. Her parties were frequent, lavish, and well attended. These festive banquets were given both at her Denver home and at Avoca, a 204-acre ranch just south of Denver that the Browns purchased in 1895.

Margaret sent this glamorous photo of herself to relatives in Hannibal. Even her handwriting had an artistic flourish. *(The Denver Public Library, Western History Collection)*

Margaret takes a last look at an elegantly set dinner table before the guests arrive. She often entertained to raise money for charitable causes. *(Colorado Historical Society)*

Nearly eight hundred people, including several members of European royalty, showed up for one Brown outdoor gala. That evening Margaret had expensive Oriental rugs spread on the lawn for her guests to stand on. Decorative lawn tents assembled for the occasion were filled with delicious delicacies, and three different bands played throughout the evening.

Margaret and J.J. were also ardent supporters of charitable causes.

Over the years, the couple gave generously to Catholic Charities and also raised funds for the city's Cathedral of the Immaculate Conception and St. Joseph's Hospital. J. J. also made annual Christmas donations to St. Vincent's Orphan Asylum. He kept his generosity out of the press but made certain that each child received a new outfit as well as something for fun, such as a sled or skates. It is not known whether his wife's concern for destitute mining families influenced his choice of charities, but most of the orphans at St. Vincent's were miners' children. J. J. supposedly once said that he "felt he owed these children something for the loss of their fathers in the mines."[7]

While Margaret's life might have sometimes seemed like a whirlwind of fancy gowns and parties, there was actually much more to this woman than social functions. She never looked down on those who had less, and she worked tirelessly for a number of Denver charities. Unlike many society matrons who viewed volunteer work as an obligation, Margaret put her heart into whatever she did.

In 1898, she served as chairperson of the Denver Women's Club Art and Literature Committee, raising money to buy books and magazines for the club's reading room as well as to provide art instruction and supplies to public schools. She even began teaching. Her evening course on the architecture and highlights of London was enjoyable and well attended.

Margaret was especially proud of her involvement in the River Front Park Project, in which she helped have a playground and summer school built for over five hundred children who otherwise would not have had a place to play or learn. The club secretary perhaps best summed up the lasting effect this endeavor had on Margaret and others when she wrote in the club's yearbook:

Thousands throng the streets of Denver for the opening of the Cathedral of the Immaculate Conception. Margaret and J.J. raised money to help build the church and worshiped there for many years. *(Colorado Historical Society)*

The experiences of the summer have left a deep impression not only on the children in whose colorless lives has been brought a new and wholesome element, but upon the women who in serving here have come to know the people in their comfortless homes and have entered into the almost hopeless struggle of their lives. They have been brought in touch with conditions that call for charity when justice might avail. Through the work of the River Front we have been brought face to face with the burning questions of the day, and we cannot lightly turn from them again.[8]

67

Along with a group of other dedicated women, Margaret kept on working for what she believed in, and in time their efforts began to have noticeable results. The Denver Women's Club was credited with applying sufficient political pressure to bring about more extensive child-labor laws. Additional traveling libraries were established, and larger numbers of women were serving on school boards than ever before.

Margaret Brown was often at the forefront of important movements for change. This was especially evident when she was appointed head of the organizing committee for the bazaar held as a fundraiser for St. Joseph's Hospital. Margaret poured all her time and energy into the project, soliciting donations from merchants throughout the city and arranging for booths that offered a tempting array of dishes and the finest delicacies Denver candymakers could produce. The bazaar was a phenomenal success, raising more money than had been anticipated as well as garnering valuable support for the hospital's much-needed enlargement.

The local media credited Margaret with the results. Even during the preparations, the *Denver Republic* reported that Mrs. Brown "is so busy that it is almost impossible to find her anywhere, and whatever success the fair attains will be due in no small degree to her energy." Noting her unique organizational ability in bringing diverse elements together, the *Denver Times* further reported that Margaret's "organization of various committees . . . has been remarkably successful."[9]

Margaret's sense of social responsibility as well as her talent for organization did not go unnoticed by the church, and she was continually requested to assist with various Catholic fundraisers. It seemed natural, therefore, that she would be asked to run a second fair just two years later. As always, her approach was inclusive, and she invited women of several other faiths to her home to participate in this worthy community cause.

She relied on her creativity in devising unusual booths that would be certain to draw people to the fair. One winner was a booth in which dolls, which were either handmade or donated by celebrities, were to be auctioned. Among those who donated dolls were the wives of presidents William McKinley and Theodore Roosevelt and presidential candidate William Jennings Bryan. The fair drew people from throughout the state, and Margaret added another event to her list of successes.

While Margaret was raising money for charitable causes, she insisted on remaining active in politics. Delighted that Colorado women had won the right to vote in 1893, she threw her money and support behind politicians who favored woman suffrage on a national level. And even though she was still active in her church, Margaret was among the women whom church officials cited as going too far in the struggle for women's rights. A priest, Father O'Ryan, expressed this view when he addressed the members of the Denver Philosophical Society, saying:

I would like to see the question [of woman suffrage] put to a vote again in Colorado and have it voted down. I voted for woman suffrage when it was presented to us, but now I feel that I ought to throw a white sheet about myself and stand in front of the church door and do penance for it. It is working harm to the women of the state. I have been shocked to see them engage in political work as they have, in precinct canvassing and on election day at the polls. The women are losing their womanhood through it.[10]

Margaret took the criticism in stride and did not waver either in her political activism or in her devotion to the church. In July 1906, she launched what would prove to be one of her most spectacular church fundraisers, the Carnival of Nations. She was ahead of her time in that she embraced Denver's ethnic diversity and often devised projects that included people of all races and beliefs. The Carnival of Nations was her hope for a community effort that reflected the idea of America as a rich tapestry of cultures.

She planned to have various booths representing different countries and ethnic groups. Those staffing them would dress in the traditional garb of a particular place and sell typical food and souvenirs. Among those participating were Mexicans, Italians, Irish, and African Americans.

Margaret also decided to include Indians and Chinese. At the time, the broadest ethnic prejudice was directed at these people, and her decision was highly controversial. But she stood firm on her plan to include them and argued that those who disagreed should come to the fair and learn more about what they obviously didn't know. As was true of most of her undertakings, the international fair was extremely successful. Some people even claimed that "the carnival [was] to Denver what the World's Fair was to St. Louis."[11]

Besides her work for the church, Margaret also raised money for a juvenile justice system through which troubled boys could be rehabilitated rather than just imprisoned. Her work in this area focused on her lifelong belief that by helping children one could change the world. In the circle in which she moved, she knew many people of considerable wealth and influence, and she never hesitated to call on them to help her achieve her goals.

But despite Margaret's broad popularity both at home and abroad,

A group of Ute men and women in Denver pose for a studio portrait. Margaret included Indians in her community projects, to the disdain of others. *(The Denver Public Library, Western History Collection)*

there was one group that failed to appreciate her. This was the elite old guard of Denver society known as the Sacred 36. Led by Mrs. Crawford Hill, this conservative group was put off by Margaret's liberal politics and her outspokenness on various issues.

In their estimation, Margaret had done the unthinkable. She had continually challenged a woman's role in polite society by taking on controversial causes and questioning the status quo. As a result, the Sacred 36 excluded the Browns from their social gatherings and often made Margaret the object of their stinging remarks and jokes.

The group was especially critical of Margaret's relationship to the

The Sacred 36 enjoying an exclusive banquet at the Denver Country Club.
(*Colorado Historical Society*)

press, which she carefully cultivated. Margaret Brown was actually media savvy before it was chic to be so. She purposely invited newspaper people to her galas and fundraisers, kept them abreast of interesting events in her life, and even sent them photos of herself in her most fantastic outfits. With only a few exceptions, she received favorable coverage. Some historical observers think that Margaret eventually became legendary because the press liked her and wrote about her endeavors in a positive light. However, her courting of the press in an era when newspaper coverage and reporters were not considered part of refined society made her seem vulgar to the Sacred 36.

There may also have been other reasons for Margaret's exclusion.

Margaret's sister Helen, the Tobin family beauty, signed this photo of herself
"Admiringly yours." Obviously, she did not agree with the Sacred 36's opinion
of Margaret. *(The Denver Public Library, Western History Collection)*

She never tried to hide that she was Irish Catholic. As noted by the historian Byron R. Bronstein, who organized the J.J. Brown papers for the Colorado Historical Society: "[Margaret] and J.J. were Irish Catholics. . . . Perhaps their ethnicity had something to do with the lack of early acceptance by white Anglo-Saxon Protestant Denver society."[12]

While stories about Margaret's life portray her as clamoring for the Sacred 36's acceptance, that depiction isn't accurate. Margaret and J.J. were not outsiders looking in on Denver's upper crust; they were the essence of a new, bolder mainstream that was shaping Denver society. At this point in her life, Margaret had already grown too concerned with the social injustices around her to care very much about a small group's snobbery. She was now more interested in feeding hungry children than in receiving an invitation to a fancy dinner party.

CHAPTER 7

Heroine of the *Titanic*

S HAKESPEARE WROTE, "All that glisters is not gold," and in some ways this proved especially true for the Brown family as time passed. As always, the energetic Mrs. Brown kept busy traveling and working for social causes and charity benefits. Both children attended Sacred Heart, a Catholic school in Denver, before going off to boarding schools in France and elsewhere. J.J. was rarely home, frequently traveling to various parts of the United States and Mexico to see to his mining investments and real estate holdings.

The couple had grown apart emotionally and frequently disagreed on issues central to their lives. Although Margaret and J.J. now had the money to make their dreams come true, they no longer shared a common dream. In addition to working for more equitable conditions in Colorado, Margaret wanted to spend time in Europe. She was especially taken with France, often noting that she enjoyed its people, language, and culture. She helped to create the Denver branch of the Alliance Française, a club where people came together to practice their French and study interesting aspects of the country.

J.J., on the other hand, liked Ireland more than France, though he really preferred spending most of his time in the United States. Those closest to him felt that instead of travel he yearned for a quiet life that centered around his family and mining friends.

The pair also disagreed on how to raise the children. J.J. believed that young children should be with their parents rather than sent away to school. He liked the local schools and resented the fact that by 1900 their son, Lawrence, who was thirteen, no longer had a bedroom in the house. "They went to Paris without my consent," J.J. wrote to an associate, "as I had to allow Mrs. Brown to do as she pleased in this as well as other matters." He further confided to a friend, "She has ruined [the children] for any earthly use."[1]

In those days, it wasn't uncommon for affluent couples to have separate bedrooms, and J.J. spent an increasing amount of time by himself. His room was on the north side of the house near his office, so he and Margaret were easily able to avoid each other. There were periods when, because of their individual travel plans, they didn't see each other for months.

J.J.'s health problems further affected the marriage. Both rheumatism and heart trouble prevented him from working as vigorously as he had when he was younger, and this made him extremely irritable and difficult to be around. He had also become a heavy drinker, which only worsened his health and marital concerns.

Sadly, there were still other strains on the Browns' already tense relationship. J.J. was known to have dalliances with other women, and these occasionally became public. In 1904, the newspapers carried reports of how forty-eight-year-old J.J. Brown had seduced a twenty-two-year-old named Maude Call. The woman's husband blamed J.J. for ruining their marriage and sued the millionaire miner for fifty thousand dollars.

No one is smiling in this somewhat strained portrait of Margaret and her family.
(The Denver Public Library, Western History Collection)

As the Brown children grew older, there seemed to be less reason for Margaret and J.J. to stay together. Their daughter, Helen, later recalled that her parents frequently fought. "The terrible situation which existed between Mother and Father was the tragedy of my childhood," she noted.[2]

77

Acknowledging that their marriage was failing, the Browns separated in 1909. Divorce was out of the question, as both Margaret and J.J. were Catholic and it was against their church's doctrine. From then on, however, they lived apart. Margaret kept the Pennsylvania Avenue home and received a monthly allowance and some stock dividends. J.J. now spent much of his time in California and Arizona. Margaret rented out the Denver house, as she was usually also away. Although she still wasn't accepted by Denver's Sacred 36, she soon became a welcome and frequent guest in the homes of far more prestigious New York society families, such as the Astors, Vanderbilts, and Whitneys.

Margaret often traveled abroad with these well-known, affluent Americans, accompanied by her daughter. While she and Helen were in Switzerland with the Astors and others, she hired a tutor to teach her to yodel. Margaret soon became so proficient at it that she was frequently asked to entertain at parties and was sometimes even referred to as "the American Warbler."

Helen also received a good deal of attention on these trips. A striking red-headed beauty, she had been brought up with every advantage. As a young girl she had been exposed to music, art, and the classics at exclusive European boarding schools. Following graduation, she continued her studies at the Sorbonne in Paris. She effortlessly drew people to her wherever she went and was invited to all the important social events of the year. There was never a shortage of young men, either in Europe or America, wishing to escort her.

Now in her early twenties, Helen was expected to marry, and she seemed to especially like a handsome young man named George Benziger. He was from a prominent Swiss Catholic family that was well established in the U.S. publishing industry. Helen, however,

Margaret and Helen with friends in Littleton, Colorado. Always in fashion, Helen wears a hat elaborately decorated with flowers, while Margaret stands an umbrella upright. *(The Denver Public Library, Western History Collection)*

tended to be more conservative than her mother, and she was not about to rush into anything.

Her brother, Lawrence, on the other hand, was less reserved. At times, his relationship with his father was hardly ideal. J.J. took a dim view of his son's behavior after Lawrence was asked to leave Phillips Exeter Academy in New Hampshire over an incident in which he and some friends had acted rowdily in public. Both J.J. and Margaret hoped that Lawrence would eventually attend Yale University, but that never happened.

By the time he was in his early twenties, Lawrence had fallen in love. He was captivated by an attractive woman name Eileen Horton,

Lawrence Brown was twenty-four years old when he married for the first time. His twenty-one-year-old bride, Eileen Horton, affectionately called him Laurie. *(Colorado Historical Society)*

whom he met while vacationing with his mother and sister in Grand Lake, Colorado. Margaret liked Eileen, although she felt that her son was not ready for marriage. While there was little else that she and J.J. agreed on by then, J.J. strongly urged his son to complete his education or at least try to secure his financial future before marrying.

But Larry couldn't wait. Two years after meeting Eileen, and no closer to being established in business, he married her. Neither of his parents was present for the occasion. J.J. was too angry at what he viewed as his son's rashness to attend the ceremony, and Margaret was away in Europe at the time.

J.J. temporarily cut Larry off financially following the wedding, and the young groom was forced to take a daytime mining job in Colorado. This proved to be the first of more than twenty jobs that he had during the next decade. At various times he was employed as a bricklayer, a lumber salesman, and a real estate agent. On several occasions Lawrence tried to go into business for himself, but none of these ventures ever really took off.

About a year after Larry and Eileen were married they had a son, whom they named Lawrence Jr. but called Pat. This was the sick child Margaret was on her way to see when she boarded the ill-fated *Titanic* in April 1912. Fortunately, the baby recovered, and Lawrence was relieved to learn that his mother had survived the ocean ordeal. Helen had also feared for her mother's safety. That Margaret was safe and in good spirits was evident from the following letter Helen received from her at the time:

My Dear Child,

   After being brined, salted, and pickled in mid ocean I am now high and dry. . . . I was the first one to leave a message at the Marconie on board the *Carpathia,* but the system was so glutted they couldn't get through. . . . I didn't think anyone knew I was on board. . . . I have had flowers, letters, telegrams from people until I am befuddled. They are petitioning Congress to give me a medal and to inscribe my name on a monument erected in New York Harbor. If I must call a specialist to examine my head it is due to the title of Heroine of the *Titanic.* . . . I am now struggling with reporters. . . .

Love,

Mother[3]

As "Heroine of the *Titanic*," Margaret Brown became the toast of Denver, and the city's Sacred 36 now eagerly embraced her. Society matrons who had once scorned her welcomed her home, and even Mrs. Crawford Hill gave a luncheon in her honor. But it's doubtful that their acceptance meant very much to Margaret, who had other things on her mind. Surviving a tragedy of the *Titanic*'s magnitude had put things in perspective for her. This was indicated in her reply when a reporter asked her about the gowns, cash, and expensive jewelry she had lost on the *Titanic*. "I feel worse over my four cases of pictures and the models of the ruins of Rome that I was taking to the museum in Denver than over my clothes and gems," she said.[4]

Margaret saw things on the *Titanic* that profoundly affected her. She had obviously been moved by how the socialite couple Ida and Isidor Straus had perished, and she frequently told their story. Margaret had looked on as Ida Straus boarded a lifeboat and then got out in order to remain on the ship with her husband. Apparently, Mrs. Straus was not about to abandon the man she had loved and with whom she had spent her life. "Noble woman!" Margaret noted in describing Ida Straus's actions. "I will never forget her as I saw her last, holding fast to her husband's arm as the two walked along the deck of that sinking ship."[5]

Following the *Titanic* tragedy, Margaret wasn't content to bask in the glory of the recognition she received. Believing that many lives had been lost because of negligence and poor conduct on the part of the ship's staff, she hoped to testify before the U.S. Senate committee investigating the incident. Knowing that those who perished could never be brought back, Margaret longed to see justice done for them.

But she was never called on to testify, despite her valued role in the

Margaret's heroic role in the *Titanic* tragedy made her a celebrity. The Denver Women's Club even petitioned Congress to give her a medal. *(Colorado Historical Society)*

rescue efforts. Only a handful of women were asked, and most of them sent in sworn written statements instead of appearing in person. In the early 1900s, women were still expected to act demurely and know their place. Even though the majority of *Titanic* survivors were female, their bravery and resourcefulness in saving themselves and others obviously didn't change that.

Despite these societal restrictions, Margaret's account of the *Titanic* tragedy was still loudly heard. That's because her heroism resulted in a press corps eager to write down her every word on any subject. Suddenly, large numbers of people were anxious to listen to Mrs. Brown and take seriously what she had to say. At last, she had a forum from which to argue for the social causes in which she believed, and many women and children profited from her efforts.

First she petitioned Congress to reform maritime law. After the *Titanic* disaster, she felt that the practice of breaking up families to put women and children in lifeboats first didn't benefit females in the long run. She thought that drowning was no worse than being left destitute with no way to care for one's children. "Their husbands [on the *Titanic*] went down to practically painless deaths," she said in explaining her position, "while they are left to suffer living deaths."[6] When told that as the weaker sex, women were entitled to special treatment in a maritime crisis, Margaret replied, "If the women ask for equal rights on land, they should concede equal rights at sea."[7]

As might be expected, Margaret had some very definite ideas about how women could achieve equality on land. She wanted to see females step out of their traditional roles as homemakers both to own businesses and to work as high-level managers in male-dominated industries. The mining industry was among Margaret's first targets, and she formed a feminist group that became active in the Little Jonny mine, where J.J. had made his fortune.

Margaret worked with added fervor for equal rights for women in the political arena. She felt that women should be allowed to serve in the armed forces and fight on the battlefield alongside men. She always said that she knew more than one woman who could shoot a rifle as well or better than any man.

Margaret knew that to achieve these and other goals, women had to make their voices heard at the ballot box. She firmly believed that true equality would never be achieved until all American women had the right to vote. She began devoting much of her time to organizing letter-writing campaigns, boycotts, and demonstrations toward that end. Always in demand as a speaker, Margaret Brown lectured throughout the country, describing what had occurred on the *Titanic* while relating it to the feminist cause she championed.

As before, she also continued to give generously of her time and funds when particularly abusive situations were brought to her attention. That's what happened in 1914 in the mining town of Ludlow, just outside Denver. In this company-owned town, workers and their families had been living in crude, unsanitary shacks. When they went on strike to demand better living conditions, the United Mine Workers of America helped set up tents in which the families could live until the dispute was resolved.

Margaret supported the union's efforts morally and financially, and so she was horrified to learn that the mining company had called in the Colorado militia to deal with the strikers. In what became known as the Ludlow Massacre, the soldiers fired into the crowd, killing seven men, and set fire to the tent city where the strikers were staying.

Members of the Colorado National Guard were called in to suppress the miners' strike at Ludlow. *(The Denver Public Library, Western History Collection)*

Numerous women and children died in the fire. The ruthless killings infuriated Margaret and increased her determination to continue fighting for decent working and living conditions.

She used her organizational skills to do what she could for the Ludlow miners and their families. In the aftermath of the crisis, she helped arrange for a group of trained nurses and relief workers to provide immediate aid, and she sent boxes of shoes and warm clothing to be distributed.

As chairperson of the newly formed Women's Relief Committee, Margaret Brown worked with the Denver United Garment Workers Union, the Women's Peace Association, and the Young Women's Christian Association to arrange a benefit concert to raise money for the Ludlow victims. Using her own funds to rent a hall, she convinced a number of entertainers to perform free. All the proceeds went for supplies for the destitute mining families.

Margaret often spoke of the strike when addressing various audiences. Talking about it before a large crowd at the woman suffrage headquarters in New York, she stressed that mining conditions like those that sparked the Ludlow strike were prevalent throughout the country. She now strongly advocated a "rights for all" movement to bring about important changes, including vastly improved work environments and universal suffrage for women.

Believing that suffrage and the politics behind the Ludlow incident were inseparable, Margaret felt the best way to effect change would be through public office. So in 1914 she became one of the first women to run for the U.S. Congress. Though she lost the election, she refused to give up. She later joined a group of feminists who petitioned President Calvin Coolidge to support an Equal Rights Amendment.

Margaret distributed this photo to the press to launch her campaign for Congress. Her candidacy made an important statement for women. *(Colorado Historical Society)*

Although he opposed women's right to vote, President Calvin Coolidge is seen here with the Republican women who helped in his presidential campaign. *(Library of Congress)*

Margaret Brown's actions served as an important example of what a strong woman could accomplish in what was still very much a man's world. A Denver newspaper later described the driving force behind her deeds: "She was a definite fearless personality. She knew what she wanted and went after it, and seldom failed of her goal."[8]

As the years passed, Margaret continued meeting challenges on her own terms, never allowing middle age or gender to stop her. She once told a journalist:

Why should a woman be mildewed at forty? That's the best time to start a real career. Assuming she is a mother, her children are launched by that time; if a childless wife, she has probably mothered her husband's activities to the point of success; if wage-earning and responsibility occupied her early years, she has won success and can afford to take her breath and look around a little.[9]

It seemed certain that Margaret Brown was not going to slow down, and indeed she was destined to remain in the limelight for years to come.

CHAPTER 8

In Later Years

MARGARET BROWN WAS admired by people who read about her or heard her speak, but unfortunately her immediate family did not always join in that admiration. There were some particularly tense moments between Margaret and her estranged husband. Although he continued to support her, J. J. felt that Margaret was far too extravagant, and he frequently warned her to limit her spending.

In the 1963 film *The Unsinkable Molly Brown,* the couple reunite after the sinking of the *Titanic,* but that did not happen in real life. Actually, the Browns never again lived together. When J. J. heard that the press was calling his wife "the Unsinkable Mrs. Brown," he reportedly said, "She's too mean to sink."[1]

Just as Margaret pursued her own interests after their separation, J. J. did the same. When able to take some time off from work, he frequently returned to Leadville to visit friends and relatives. J. J. always preferred his mining buddies to the society gentlemen he met in Denver and abroad. In all likelihood, he would have moved back there if his doctor had not warned him that the town's high altitude and harsh winters would worsen his health. J. J. wrote in a letter to his son, Larry:

Leadville is very quiet but I wished a thousand times that I could withstand her winters and then here I would stay forever as long as I could live. . . . O if I could only stand the cold of old Leadville.[2]

J. J. spent time with a number of different women through the years. Occasionally, these relationships grew troublesome, as in 1919, when an actress named Sabra Simpson sued him for breach of promise. Simpson claimed that she had lived with J. J. for a time with the understanding that they would marry soon. In response, J. J. said that he and Simpson were never more than friends.

Simpson was probably after J. J.'s money, but there was actually less of it left than she and most other people thought. Through the years Margaret and J. J. had helped quite a few of their relatives start businesses, buy homes, and educate their children. They also provided their own children with an ongoing supply of cash whenever necessary. J. J. traveled extensively through the West, acquiring and managing mines for various concerns, but he never again made the sums he had made in the 1890s. By the 1920s, this resulted in some bitter arguments between Margaret and J. J. over finances, and at one point J. J. even told his son, "Your mother is my worst enemy."[3]

Meanwhile, the Brown children navigated their own relationships as best they could. Helen Brown married George Benziger in April 1913. She chose to have a quiet ceremony in New York rather than in Denver. Unlike her mother, Helen was an extremely private person who shunned publicity. She wanted her wedding to be meaningful for her and the groom, not a field day for the press. J. J. attended the wedding, but Margaret was in Germany at the time and did not make it back for the ceremony. Since she liked her new son-in-law, some

Despite his poor health in later years, J.J. always appeared handsome and distinguished.
(The Denver Public Library, Western History Collection)

suspect that she may not have wanted to risk an unpleasant exchange with J.J. Helen and George had two sons in the years that followed. James George Benziger was born on March 31, 1914, and his brother, George Peter Joseph Adelrich Benziger (known as Peter), was born on December 26, 1917.

Lawrence's marriage did not go as smoothly, and he and his wife, Eileen, divorced in 1915. Margaret was extremely upset about the breakup. The couple had two children, a son and a daughter. Margaret strongly encouraged them to get back together, and to her relief, the couple remarried in 1917. By then the United States had entered World War I. Larry enlisted in the army and eventually rose to the rank of captain.

His mother acted patriotically as well. As soon as the war broke out, Margaret offered to convert the Newport, Rhode Island, house she rented into a hospital for wounded military personnel. Although that didn't occur, the house was later used by the Newport Chapter of the American Red Cross. In the meantime, Margaret headed for France to assist in the overseas war effort. She hired two American nurses to accompany her and arrived with several cases of medical supplies and equipment. Along with a number of other American volunteers, she helped establish a relief station for soldiers. She had always loved France, and now her fluency in the language proved especially useful.

Her work didn't stop there. She joined the American Committee for Devastated France (called CARD, after its French name), a volunteer effort that was formed to help rebuild war-torn areas behind the front lines. It was a massive undertaking, but one that Margaret relished. She became a CARD director, serving as a much-needed link between French government officials and the people in the areas

During World War I, Lawrence was an infantry captain in the American Expeditionary Forces. He served honorably in Europe and was wounded in a mustard gas attack in September 1918. *(Colorado Historical Society)*

involved. Besides supervising building reconstruction, Margaret made certain that food, clothing, blankets, and other vital items were promptly distributed where needed. Looking ahead, she also worked on construction plans for new and enlarged schools, libraries, and medical centers. As a token of the nation's appreciation, her name was inscribed on a plaque honoring American volunteers who worked selflessly for France's good.

After returning home, Margaret continued her war-related humanitarian efforts. Following the war's end in 1918, she worked with soldiers who had been blinded during the war, helping them learn how to live on their own and earn a living. She even tried to have some books by Mark Twain, the famous author from her hometown of Hannibal, Missouri, set in Braille so that the men could enjoy these literary treasures.

At times, Margaret seemed to overflow with energy and goodwill. "If I were requested to personify perpetual activity," a New York reporter wrote, "I believe I'd name Mrs. James J. Brown, the Newport social figure, suffragette, [and] patriot."[4]

While Margaret was still spry and on the lookout for new projects, J.J. had taken a downward turn. His health deteriorated to the point that he had to be hospitalized in Los Angeles in 1921. He sent a telegram to his daughter, Helen, in New York, asking her to come to California. Helen went, and remained with her father until he was well enough to travel and go back east with her. It was a difficult time for Helen, who knew that both her two young children in New York and her ailing father in California needed her. She was also aware that her father would have preferred to stay in the West, but she firmly believed that he would be better off living with her.

Helen Brown Benziger with her young sons, James and Peter. *(Colorado Historical Society)*

Even as a young girl, Helen had been particularly close to her father. Now she felt it was unfair that J.J., who had always been extremely generous to the entire family, was not surrounded by loved ones while he was so ill. Helen also believed that her mother was more at fault for the marriage's breakup than J.J., and she once wrote of Margaret:

She was not entirely to blame in the trouble with Father, not originally, because he was difficult, hot-tempered in the extreme and hard to please. . . . But whereas he tried and did mend his ways

97

and controlled himself more and more as he grew older . . . she succumbed more and more to what became . . . a ruling passion in her life.[5]

Helen wanted to make it up to her father and tried to nurse him back to health at her New York home. Unfortunately, by then he was too ill for her to succeed. J.J. was admitted to a local hospital and, after suffering two heart attacks there, died on September 5, 1922. He was alone at the time of his death. Helen reached the hospital less than a half hour later. Although J.J. and Margaret had fought for years, shortly before he died, J.J. asked his children to look out for their mother.

Margaret had kept a soft spot in her heart for J.J. When asked about him years later, she said:

Let me say here that I've been all over the world. I have known more or less intimately the greatest people in the world from the kings down, or up, as one cares to view them, and I've never met a finer, bigger, more worthwhile man than J.J. Brown. In spite of certain qualities in our natures which made companionship impossible between us, I salute his memory and claim him to have been without a peer.[6]

Life for all the Browns was more difficult without J.J. He had always been a prudent businessman, so Margaret was shocked to learn that he had died without a valid will. Sadly, that set the stage for further family friction. Since Margaret was still legally his wife at the time of his death, she hoped to be appointed executor of his estate. Her chil-

Pitted against her own children over J.J.'s estate, Margaret testifies in a court battle. Her daughter, Helen, once said that as youngsters she and Larry thought they had the best mother in the world. *(The Denver Public Library, Western History Collection)*

dren, however, were against this, and the court denied her request. When her lawyers learned that large sums of money had been signed over to Helen and Lawrence not long before J.J. died, Margaret felt certain that her son-in-law, George Benziger, was behind it. Her daughter deeply resented her insinuations.

Court battles between Margaret and her children over the division of J.J.'s estate tore the family apart. Lawrence and Helen stood firm in their belief that their mother spent money too freely, giving more to charitable causes than she could afford. Lawrence further suspected that his mother was incapable of properly managing sizable amounts of cash.

Although in the end Margaret was left with a healthy trust fund, it was not adequate for her to live as she had in earlier times. After falling behind in the rent, she was forced to give up her house in Newport. While as a young girl she had wanted money to help her family, toward the end of her life it was money that kept her family at odds.

Nevertheless, she continued to lead a full life. She had many friends, traveled, and remained a champion of social, political, and artistic causes internationally. She was back in the newspapers in 1926 when she returned to her birthplace for the dedication of a statue of Tom Sawyer and Huckleberry Finn in honor of Mark Twain. At the time, Margaret told reporters that she was busy working on her own life story. She said that she was thinking about calling it *The Course of Human Events,* but the text was never completed.

In 1927, Margaret became interested in historic preservation. When the cottage of the poet-journalist Eugene Field in Denver was about to be demolished, she purchased it and had it moved to a safe location in

The Tom and Huck statue at the foot of Cardiff Hill in Hannibal, Missouri, in honor of Mark Twain. *(Mark Twain Museum)*

Margaret with a group of young girls whom she worked with in a fundraising effort. They put on a show to save the Eugene Field cottage. *(Molly Brown House)*

the city's Washington Park. She placed it next to the Wynken, Blynken, and Nod fountain, which was named for Field's popular children's poem. She actively supported other preservation endeavors as well.

Margaret also spent quite a bit of time in France, which had always been her home away from home. There she continued studying drama and successfully re-created some of the roles made famous by the actress Sarah Bernhardt. In May 1929, she received the Palm of the Academy of France for her achievements in the dramatic arts. In April 1932, she was again honored. This time she was given the prestigious French Legion of Honor award for all she did for the country during and after the war and for promoting positive Franco-American relations.

Even as she grew older, Margaret was the subject of numerous stories concerning her personal life. It is not known how much truth these stories contained. There were newspaper reports suggesting that she planned to adopt two children, a boy and a girl. Though she helped pay for a young boy's education, she did not adopt him or anyone else.

It was also reported that Margaret was engaged to a French duke. As it turned out, his title was extinct and the wedding never took place. That was one of the rare times Margaret was romantically linked to a gentleman following J.J.'s death. Though undeniably intelligent and witty, Margaret was often the center of attention at a time when a man did not want a wife who was considered more important than he was. It was also noted in society circles that Margaret had "come out so strong for suffrage" that some would-be suitors felt intimidated.[7] None of this seemed to bother her. She always put fighting for equality above being courted and had more than her share of friends.

Some of these friends claimed that Margaret had more lives than a cat. After surviving the *Titanic,* she later escaped unharmed from a serious fire in the Breakers Hotel in Palm Beach, Florida, where she was staying. It seemed as if nothing frightened Margaret Brown. As she once wrote about herself:

I am a daughter of adventure. This means I never experience a dull moment and must be prepared for any eventuality. I never know when I may go up in an airplane and come down with a crash, or go motoring and climb a pole, or go off for a walk in the twilight and return all mussed up in an ambulance. That's my arc, as the astrologers would say. It's a good one, too, for a person who had rather make a snap-out than a fade-out of life.[8]

The Breakers, where Margaret often stayed, is a magnificent resort situated on 140 acres of oceanfront property. Founded in 1896, the five-star resort is listed on the National Register of Historic Places. *(The Breakers)*

After 1929, Margaret divided her time between living at New York's Barbizon Hotel (a haven for actresses) and traveling abroad and to the West. She also began to heal her relationship with her daughter. Like J.J., Margaret loved returning to Leadville. She never forgot her happy days there as a young mother. She still had family and friends there, and always enjoyed reminiscing with them. Margaret

Despite her advancing years, Margaret Brown's love of travel never waned.
(Colorado Historical Society)

Margaret's last home, the Barbizon Hotel, has been a New York landmark for more than seventy years. *(Barbizon Hotel)*

Though Margaret needed a cane toward the end of her life, she still remained active. *(The Denver Public Library, Western History Collection)*

especially liked going out to Twin Lakes to enjoy the scenery where she and J.J. had honeymooned.

The Depression of the late 1920s and 1930s left families across the country in poverty. Margaret saw its devastating effects firsthand in 1932, when she visited relatives in Leadville and realized that many of

ABOVE LEFT: Actress Tammy Grimes played Margaret in the hit Broadway musical *The Unsinkable Molly Brown*. Margaret, however, was nothing like the comical character portrayed here. *(The New York Public Library)* ABOVE RIGHT: Kathy Bates was the actress chosen to play Margaret Brown in James Cameron's 1997 Oscar-winning movie *Titanic*. *(Paramount Pictures and 20th Century Fox)*

the town's children had no warm winter clothes. She had sent Christmas gifts to Leadville's youth before, and now she wanted to do more. She bought a large number of children's mittens, mufflers, and boots to be given out as holiday presents.

Margaret never lived to see the joy and comfort she brought to Leadville that year. Although she had previously survived several small strokes, she died of a massive stroke on October 26, 1932. One of Helen's sons later remembered that his mother received a phone call in the middle of the night from the Barbizon Hotel manager, informing her that her mother had died in her sleep. Margaret was sixty-five years old at the time. Her generosity lived on, however; her nephew Ted Brown distributed the holiday gifts among the children of Leadville.

Although Margaret Brown had been well known and liked in both Leadville and Denver, her final resting place was not in the West. Instead, she was buried next to J.J. in Holy Rood cemetery in Westbury, Long Island, New York. There were stories that Margaret had bequeathed substantial sums of money to various individuals, but there was actually very little left.

The flighty title character in the 1960s play and film *The Unsinkable Molly Brown* did not reflect the real woman. The true Margaret Brown gave the world something far more lasting and important than these fictionalized accounts depicted. The essence of her life may best have been summed up by historical scholar Tom Noel when he said that Margaret Tobin Brown was "a model of how a poor, uneducated woman from a denigrated ethnic group could rise to the top in a man's world. . . . She was an early feminist, preservationist, and philanthropist."[9]

Margaret Brown had the courage to stand up for what she believed in, even when it was unpopular to do so. While other affluent women were still sipping tea in their parlors, she strove to change society. "It isn't . . . what you have," she once said, "but who you are that counts."[10] Clearly, Margaret Brown was a woman ahead of her time who made her life count.

Aftermath

What Happened to the House?

Like its owner, Margaret Brown's Denver home has an interesting story. Although Margaret owned the house until she died, she didn't always live in it. When the Browns traveled extensively in 1902, they rented it to Governor James Orman and his wife, who held various social events as well as state affairs during their stay.

After the Browns separated in 1909, Margaret began renting out the house on a regular basis. In 1926, she stopped a tenant from renting rooms to boarders — only to later turn it into a boardinghouse herself.

When Margaret died in 1932, there was an outstanding mortgage of $3,100 on the house. The neighborhood was no longer as fashionable as it had been when the Browns moved there, and it was also the end of the Great Depression. The dwelling was appraised for only $6,000. The furnishings were sold for $200 in an auction, and the house was sold in 1933 for $5,000. In the years that followed, it changed hands several more times. While the exterior was never altered by the various owners, the interior was extensively changed.

By the late 1950s the Browns' once beautiful home had fallen into disrepair.
(The Denver Public Library, Western History Collection)

In 1958, still another owner turned it back into a boardinghouse, and by the late 1960s the city's Juvenile Court had leased it as a home for wayward girls.

Believing that the house was headed for demolition, a group of concerned citizens got together to save it. Incorporating themselves as Historic Denver, Inc., they used the media and a variety of activities to raise money to buy the house. Historic Denver, Inc., purchased it in 1971 for $80,000 and raised over twice that amount in the following decade to restore the house to its condition when Margaret Brown lived there. Now known as the Molly Brown House Museum,

Using photographs taken when Margaret lived there, the Browns' home was restored to its turn-of-the-century opulence by Historic Denver, Inc. *(Molly Brown House)*

it is open to the public and draws thousands of visitors annually. It is a fitting tribute to a woman who wanted to change things for the better while preserving what was of value from the past.

What Happened to the Children?

Lawrence Brown's remarriage to his wife Eileen didn't last, and the couple divorced for a second time in 1925. Their daughter later became a nun, while their son married and had two children.

Following his divorce, Lawrence worked in the film industry, where he met and fell in love with a twenty-two-year-old actress named Mildred Gregory. They married in 1926 and lived in California for a

A photo of the entrance of Holy Rood cemetery as it looked in 1931, a year before Margaret Brown was interred there. *(Catholic Cemeteries Diocese of Rockville Centre)*

time. Although they never had children of their own, Mildred reportedly got along quite well with her husband's children.

After leaving the film industry, Lawrence tried several other occupations before returning to mining. The couple moved back to Leadville—the town of his birth—where he eventually became director of the Colorado Mining Association. Lawrence Brown remained in Leadville until he died on April 3, 1949, at the age of sixty-one. He was buried with his parents in Holy Rood cemetery.

Helen Brown Benziger didn't share her father's and brother's enthusiasm for western mining towns and felt more at home in eastern social circles, where she was well regarded. She was a beautiful woman who kept her good looks as she matured. Throughout her life, she shunned the limelight and never tried to capitalize on her mother's fame.

Helen's son James attended Princeton University and later became a professor of English. He had three children. His brother, Peter, did well in the publishing industry, as had their father, and had five daughters.

Helen Brown Benziger died in 1970 in New York at the age of eighty-one. Her husband, George, had died a number of years earlier. Both he and Helen were buried in Long Island's Holy Rood cemetery with the other Brown family members.

What Happened to Leadville?

J.J. Brown was not the first man to make his fortune in Leadville. Others, such as industrialist Meyer Guggenheim, amassed even greater wealth. Guggenheim reluctantly accepted a half interest in two Leadville silver mines in 1881 as payment of a debt—mines that proved to be among the richest in the area. He also secured a near monopoly of Leadville's copper mines, which proved very lucrative.

Numerous individuals in related businesses also got their start in Leadville. Charles Dow worked as a reporter in the mining town before beginning his now-famous Dow Jones news service. Both Marshall Field and David May sold clothing to Leadville miners and their families prior to launching hugely successful department-store chains.

Leadville never stopped being a mining town—until February 1999, that is. That was when the last working mine, the Black Cloud, permanently shut down. The Environmental Protection Agency had determined that the site was a health hazard because of pollution buildup from years of mining. The Black Cloud's closing was viewed

Today Leadville still retains much of its original character and charm. A major part of the city has been designated as a National Historic Landmark District. *(Steve Sunday)*

by some as the end of an era. When Leadville was in its glory, nearly sixty thousand people lived there, but by the 1990s there were only about three thousand four hundred residents. Nevertheless, the town still has its Natural Mining Hall of Fame, and there are many residents who are proud of Leadville's exciting past and who refuse to give up on its future.

Chronology

1867 Margaret Tobin is born on July 18.

1877 Substantial amounts of silver are discovered in Leadville, Colorado.

1886 Margaret moves to Leadville. On September 1, she marries James Joseph (J.J.) Brown.

1887 Margaret and J.J.'s son, Lawrence Palmer, is born on August 30.

1889 Margaret and J.J.'s daughter, Catherine Ellen (known as Helen), is born on July 1.

1893 The Sherman Silver Purchase Act is repealed, plunging Leadville into an economic depression.

1894 The Brown family moves to Denver.

1902 The Browns take a lengthy international tour, renting out their Pennsylvania Avenue home to Governor James Orman and his wife.

1906 Margaret organizes the successful Carnival of Nations.

1909 Margaret and J.J. separate.

1912 The luxury ocean liner *Titanic* sinks on night of April 14–15.

1914 Margaret aids victims of Ludlow miners' strike; she runs for U.S. Congress but is defeated. When World War I breaks out, she goes to France to aid in the war effort.

1922 J.J. dies on September 5.

1927 Margaret purchases the Eugene Field House, saving it from demolition.

1929 Margaret receives the Palm of the Academy of France for her achievements in dramatic arts.

1932 Margaret receives the French Legion of Honor award.

1932 Margaret dies on October 26 at the age of sixty-five.

1999 Leadville's last working mine, the Black Cloud, permanently shuts down.

Endnotes

The references below are to books, articles, letters, and documentary films listed in the Bibliography on pages 123–25.

CHAPTER 1: "WATER, WATER, WATER"

1. Kristen Iversen, *Molly Brown: Unraveling the Myth* (Boulder, Colorado: Johnson Publishing Company, paperback edition, 1999), p. 2.

2. *The Shipbuilder* (magazine), Special Number (Midsummer 1911), p. 7.

3. Lee Davis, *Man-Made Catastrophes* (New York: Facts on File, 1993), p. 220.

4. *Molly Brown: An American Legend* (Documentary film by A&E Television Networks, 1997).

5. Christine Whitacre, *Molly Brown: Denver's Unsinkable Lady* (Denver: Historic Denver, Inc., 1984), p. 43.

6. "Mrs. J.J. Brown of Denver Adopts 3 Titanic Victims," *Denver Post* (April 27, 1912), p. 5.

7. *Denver Post* (April 27, 1912), p. 5.

8. Whitacre, p. 44.

9. Iversen, p. 24.

10. Iversen, p. 25.

11. Iversen, p. 32.

12. Daniel Allen Butler, *"Unsinkable": The Full Story* (Mechanicsburg, Pennsylvania: Stackpole Books, 1998), p. 156.

Endnotes

CHAPTER 2: A HERO AMONG US

1. Iversen, p. 35.

2. Iversen, p. 36.

3. Iversen, p. 37.

4. *Denver Post* (April 27, 1912), p. 5.

5. *Denver Post* (April 27, 1912), p. 5.

CHAPTER 3: IT STARTED IN HANNIBAL

1. Iversen, p. 74.

CHAPTER 4: LIFE IN LEADVILLE

1. Robert G. Athearn, *The Coloradans* (Albuquerque: University of New Mexico Press, 1976), p. 233.

2. Letter from Thomas E. Cahill to Lawrence Palmer Brown, January 20, 1947, Brown Family Papers.

3. Whitacre, p. 16.

4. Thomas Tonge, "Obituary," *Mining Journal* (September 1922), p. 23.

5. Iversen, p. 90.

6. Iversen, p. 90.

7. Iversen, p. 90.

8. Iversen, p. 91.

CHAPTER 5: THE NEWLYWEDS

1. Caroline Bancroft, *The Unsinkable Mrs. Brown* (Boulder, Colorado: Johnson Publishing Company, 1961), p. 8.

2. Bancroft, p. 8.

CHAPTER 6: ONWARD TO DENVER

1. Whitacre, p. 73.

2. *Unsinkable Elegance: Denver's Molly Brown House* (Documentary film by Steven Friesen for the Molly Brown House Museum, a property of Historic Denver, Inc., 1995).

3. Whitacre, p. 28.

4. Whitacre, p. 28.

5. Whitacre, p. 24.

6. Iversen, p. 118.

7. Iversen, p. 119.

8. Iversen, p. 116.

9. Iversen, p. 120.

10. Iversen, p. 127.

11. Iversen, p. 153.

12. "Historian Attacks Myths About J. J. and Molly Brown," *Rocky Mountain News Sunday Magazine* (September 10, 1989), p. 23M.

CHAPTER 7: HEROINE OF THE *TITANIC*

1. Whitacre, p. 31.

2. Whitacre, p. 38.

3. Iversen, p. 171.

4. *Denver Post* (April 27, 1912), p. 5.

5. Iversen, p. 172.

6. Whitacre, p. 48.

7. *Denver Post* (April 27, 1912), p. 5.

8. David Fridtjof Halaas, "The Many Facets of Molly Brown," *Colorado History Now* (January 1998), p. 3.

9. Iversen, p. 178.

CHAPTER 8: IN LATER YEARS

1. Whitacre, p. 46.

2. Letter from James Joseph Brown to Lawrence Palmer Brown, September 4, 1920, Brown Family Papers.

3. Whitacre, p. 54.

4. Iversen, p. 210.

5. Whitacre, p. 38.

6. Iversen, p. 217.

7. Iversen, p. 188.

8. Iversen, p. 236.

9. Tom Noel, "Molly Brown Is Still a Titanic Figure," *Denver Post* (February 8, 1998), p. 1.

10. *Denver Post* (April 27, 1912), p. 5.

Bibliography

BOOKS

Athearn, Robert G. *The Coloradans.* Albuquerque: University of New Mexico Press, 1976.

Bancroft, Caroline. *The Unsinkable Mrs. Brown.* Boulder, Colorado: Johnson Publishing Company, 1961.

Butler, Daniel Allen. *"Unsinkable": The Full Story.* Mechanicsburg, Pennsylvania: Stackpole Books, 1998.

Davis, Lee. *Man-Made Catastrophes.* New York: Facts on File, 1993.

Grinstead, Leigh A. *Molly Brown's Capitol Hill Neighborhood.* Denver: Historic Denver, Inc., 1997.

Iversen, Kristen. *Molly Brown: Unraveling the Myth.* Boulder, Colorado: Johnson Publishing Company, paperback edition, 1999.

Rogoff, David. *Denver's "Unsinkable" Molly Brown.* Boulder, Colorado: WESType Publishing Services, 1980.

Whitacre, Christine. *Molly Brown: Denver's Unsinkable Lady.* Denver: Historic Denver, Inc., 1984.

Bibliography

PERIODICALS

Brackney, Charles. "Remembering Molly Brown." *Denver Post* (April 13, 1997).

Halaas, David Fridtjof. "The Many Facets of Molly Brown." *Colorado History NOW* (Newsletter of the Colorado Historical Society, January 1998).

"Historian Attacks Myths About J.J. and Molly Brown." *Rocky Mountain News Sunday Magazine* (September 10, 1989).

"Mrs. J.J. Brown of Denver Adopts 3 Titanic Victims." *Denver Post* (April 27, 1912), p. 5.

Noel, Tom. "Molly Brown Is Still a Titanic Figure." *Denver Post* (February 8, 1998), p. 1.

The Shipbuilder (magazine), Special Number (Midsummer 1911), pp. 7–16.

Tonge, Thomas. "Obituary." *Mining Journal* (September 1922), p. 23.

LETTERS

The Brown Family Papers, Letter from James Joseph Brown to Lawrence Palmer Brown, September 4, 1920.

The Brown Family Papers, Letter from Thomas E. Cahill to Lawrence Palmer Brown, January 20, 1947.

FILMS

Molly Brown: An American Legend (Documentary film by A&E Television Networks, 1997).

Unsinkable Elegance: Denver's Molly Brown House (Documentary film by Steven Friesen for the Molly Brown House Museum, a property of Historic Denver, Inc., 1995).

Bibliography

PLACES TO VISIT

Colorado Historical Society

1300 Broadway

Denver, Colorado 80203-2137

Denver Public Library

Western History/Genealogy Division

10 West Fourteenth Avenue Parkway

Denver, Colorado 80204-2731

Molly Brown House Museum

1340 Pennsylvania Avenue

Denver, Colorado 80203-2137

INTERNET SITES

Molly Brown House Museum: www.mollybrown.com

Titanic Historical Society: www.titanic.org

Index

Note: Page numbers in **boldface** type refer to illustrations.

mining industry (*cont.*)

Ludlow Massacre, 85, **86,** 87

miners' rights and welfare, 52, **54,** 54–55, 85, 87

Molly Brown House Museum, 111–12, **112**

money:

burned in wood stove, 49–51

J.J.'s estate, 98, **99,** 100

Margaret's desire for, 35, 41, 43, 44–45

Margaret's estate, 107

Margaret's spending habits, 91, 92, 100

Nevin, Mary A. Fitzharris, 49–51

Newport (Rhode Island), 94

New York:

Barbizon Hotel, 104, **106,** 108

society, 78

Titanic survivors in, 22–24

White Star Line office, **23**

Noel, Tom, 108

Palmer, Cecilia, 51

palm reader, 3

political causes and career, 69–70, 84–89

pony cart, 61, **62**

press, 72, 84

religion. *See* Catholic church

River Front Park Project, 66–67

Rostron, Arthur H., **17,** 24–25, **25**

Sacred 36, the, 71, 72–74, **72,** 82

Schuck, Lorraine, 40

Sherman Silver Purchase Act, 56

silicosis, 55

Smith, Edward J., 8, **8,** 9

social life:

Denver, 59, 63, 65, **65,** 71, 72–74, **72,** 82

Leadville, 39, 44, 52

New York, 78

St. Joseph's Hospital, 68–69

stories about Margaret:

adopting children, 103

being poor and uneducated, 29

burning money in the wood stove, 49–51

engaged to a French duke, 103

meeting Mark Twain, 35–36

snubbed by Denver society, 63, 71–74

Straus, Ida and Isador, 82

Stumptown (Colorado), 49, **50**

suffrage, 69–70, 85, 87

Survivors' Committee, 20, 24–25, **25**

Tabor Opera House (Leadville), 38, 44, **45**

Titanic (film), **108**

Titanic (ship), 3, 6–18, **7, 20,** 81–84

accommodations, 6–8, **10**

captain, 8, **8,** 9

collision and sinking, 10–15

crew, 14–15, 27

Index